25

ANGELS

and

ASSISTS

MIGNON MYKEL

Also By Mignon Mykel

* *The Playmaker Duet (Troublemaker, Breakaway, Altercation, Holding)
can be enjoyed in one easy boxed set.*

LEEDS

25

ANGELS
and
ASSISTS

MIGNON MYKEL

PROLOGUE

DECEMBER 23RD

NINE YEARS AGO

Euphoria.

That's what this was.

The rush, the adrenaline.

And with a team that took a mid-season risk on me.

Me.

A kid from nowhere-Nebraska.

Sure, on paper, I was a semi-good bet. I played hard. Fought harder. I didn't have the support at home, with a dad who could give two shits what his sixteen-year-old did in his "spare" time—and by "spare," I meant the time I hadn't been working at the local grocery store, to help pay bills...and to support his beer habit.

But I never let the lack of someone in my corner, deter me from being the best player I could be.

Seventeen.

The first year that my life was set to change.

A month after my seventeenth birthday, I was drafted to Canada's Ontario Hockey League. While the league is considered Junior league hockey for all intents and purposes, the United States calls it semi-professional. By choosing to play in Canada on a Major

Juniors team, I was giving up my eligibility to ever play NCAA hockey.

I wasn't all that upset. I did, however, decide to play in hopes that maybe my dad would appreciate me, cheer for me...shit, maybe even just give a damn about me. Here his kid was, playing top level hockey!

Yeah.

No such luck.

Not even when I was drafted to the NHL the following June.

I wouldn't be able to tell you the last time I had a conversation with my dad, other than before he signed me off to Canada, but the draft and OHL had been my ticket to a better life. It was in Canada that I met my wife.

The Gagnons, my host family, were close to the Perri family, and even though I was working on playing professionally and Trina Perri was finishing up her final year in high school—*secondary school, excuse me*—it was easy to fall for the pretty blonde with a slight French accent.

We were married sixteen months after meeting, only four months after her seventeenth birthday.

A few months after that, I finally earned my permanent spot on the Quebec roster.

Life was fucking glorious.

For three seconds, anyway.

I didn't see a lick of NHL playing time. Sure, a few minutes every few games, but that's not what a guy looked for when it came time to play in the Show.

Times at home were starting to get stressful. Two young kids, on their own, newly married. Needless to say, the honeymoon period ended fast.

Ended even faster with the realization that we were expecting a baby.

Trina wasn't working. I wasn't actually playing. I never thought that I'd have to be a penny-pincher, not if I had an NHL contract, but when you weren't playing the minutes you wanted, and you didn't know if you were going to be re-signed, and you didn't have a non-hockey playing career to fall back on…

You pinched those pennies.

My teammates laughed; my contract and signing bonus had more zeroes behind a single digit than I knew what to do with, but without a degree, without a job to fall back on…

I wanted to be sure I was doing the right thing for my family.

Anderson was born on a sunny day in May, to parents who were hardly more than babies themselves, at all of twenty-one, and a month shy of nineteen.

I was re-signed just two weeks later.

Life seemed good; I had a new three-year contract, a little more per year than the previous years. Enough to keep us more than comfortable if, heaven forbid, something happened, and I couldn't play.

We hadn't been expecting the call downs and the call backs and the waivers. *So many damn times, this last year and a half.* Due to an oversight on the GM in Quebec's part, I played too many NHL games before being sent back to my OHL team my draft season, and thus, my professional career had begun during my first contract— marking *this* year as the year waivers kicked in for me. In layman's terms, waivers meant that any other team could grab you and take over your contract, while you were going between your contracted team's AHL and NHL teams. If you were a nobody, you were generally safe to return to your team.

If I'd been just *any* kid, I didn't think waivers were such a big deal. It sucked, yeah, to be called up and sent down; not knowing if you were playing, or when you were playing, or, shit, *where* you were playing.

But here I was—newly married, with a new baby, and I had to leave Trina in Quebec while I went wherever the hell the higher ups wanted me to go—which had been St. Paul, Minnesota. This last season, though, we got smart; we rented a condo in St. Paul so we could be together during my lengthy call-downs.

Two weeks ago, though, on my way back up on the ladder of hockey, I got the news.

I was picked up on waivers.

Now, some guys hated those words just as much as the word 'trade', but if it meant I was going to start *playing*, shit, I was all about it—and San Diego held promise. They liked my playing style, and wanted to help mold me into a bigger, better player.

And they wanted my wife, son, and me to "get comfortable."

Trina and I splurged, finding ourselves a tiny oceanside condo, rather than a rental, just outside San Diego. Cute. Little. A mortgage that wasn't going to break the bank, and one I could make work if something were to happen to my career.

The last two weeks, even though a whirlwind, made the last years seem like a bad dream.

Every home game this week, Trina and Anderson had been up in the seats, cheering the team on. They watched as I had my first major, consistent ice time—I played no less than nine minutes a game, which was a huge difference from Quebec. I had a couple hits, some note-worthy playmaking times, and even an assist.

They weren't here tonight though, and I was disappointed that I'd made my first professional goal when they weren't witness to it. With Christmas just two days away, Trina and Anderson flew back to Quebec a few nights before, and I'd join them in the morning.

...and I was going to bug the shit out of her with YouTube videos, the moment I had my wife in my arms again.

"You fucking did it!" Trevor Winksi yelled, standing up as I skated toward the bench, my gloved fist out as I prepared to go down the bench for customary post-goal fist bumps. I found a mentor in team assistant captain Trevor Winski, and it was, no doubt, because of him and his patience, that it was *me* who just lit that red light.

"Way to fucking go, kid!" he yelled again when I stepped into the bench, a grin stretched across my face. Winski grabbed my padded shoulders and shook me around. "Knew you fucking could."

I was only six years younger than him, but I didn't mind being called *kid*, not when I had a tough-as-shit player being my team BFF. He was buddy-buddy with our captain, Caleb Prescott, and therefore, with the team's goaltender, Jonny Prescott, too. 'Prescott' ran hockey here in San Diego, and I had to admit—being accepted into the personal fold, even if it was through Winski, was a pretty big accomplishment.

I didn't imagine that being Winski's friend was going to be the deciding factor on if I was staying here or shipping to Beloit, the farm team for the Enforcers club, but I didn't think it hurt to be close to those guys.

I laughed, back in the moment, as I pulled my glove off and reached for a water bottle. "It was fucking beautiful, wasn't it?"

He elbowed me as I brought the pop-top bottle to my mouth, nodding up at the Jumbotron. "I don't know, kid; you tell me."

Tilting my head back, I watched the replay, finally focusing in on the fact the arena was still yelling out cheers. Some classic rock song was blaring on the speakers, but my attention was firmly on the Jumbotron.

Hard battle in the corner. I got the puck out, but lost it. Jordan Byrd managed possession, clearing it to the other side of the zone. Bodies moved around the ice; the boards and Plexiglas rattled when players were thrown into it.

Suddenly, the puck landed by my feet.

Quick thinking. That's what the moment was.

Quick, on your feet, thinking.

I pushed the puck around the back of the net, slipping it in on the other side, just between the goalie's skate and post...

The play happened in seconds, but remembering it...

It was in slow-motion.

The type of slow-motion that had you excited and waiting for more.

I was going to remember this game for the rest of my fucking life.

***

"Leeds, back with me," John Mitchem, the team's equipment manager, said, as he reached for my elbow. We'd just walked off the bench, the team heading to the locker rooms between periods.

Two down, one to go.

"Yeah, sure," I replied, pulling off my helmet as I lumbered on my skates, behind him. I couldn't imagine what he needed me for, but I racked my brain anyway.

I didn't break a stick, and skates were moving fine.

I glanced down at my shoulder; maybe there was a snag or rip that needed to be mended from a hit I took against the boards.

Nothing.

Huh.

John walked me past the locker room, just a bit further down the hall. From here, you could still hear the excited echo of fans up above. The atmosphere was ridiculous.

It was easy to feel a high, when you played with a team with fans like San Diego's.

"What's up, John?" I asked, glancing over my shoulder as the last of the guys headed into the locker room. I wasn't sure why we'd stopped here, and not in the locker room, or, hell, even in the training room. Why in the hall?

"You need to shower and dress."

My frown was automatic. "What do you mean, I have to shower and dress?" I'd been doing well. Where the hell would the team be sending me, the day before break? Why would I be leaving in the middle of a game? Why—

"There was an accident."

***

The moment the plane's wheels touched down at Quebec City Jean Lesage, I turned my phone off airplane mode. I hadn't stopped bouncing my knee the entire flight; hadn't slept a damn wink, either. I needed to be in Quebec, and not in San Diego; I needed to be in communication with the Perris.

I wasn't sure what was worse—being the only person on the team plane, alone with my morbid thoughts and unanswered questions; or if I'd just hopped a commercial flight. At least then, I'd have been surrounded by people.

I could have connected to the WiFi.

I could have called home. Talked to someone.

But I was so fucking *helpless*, trapped on this plane. I couldn't do anything from up here in the sky.

Thank God the team plane wouldn't have to take a fuel stop. I would get to Quebec in the early morning hours.

Still hours too late.

God, Trina and Anderson had to be okay.

Please let them be okay.

The pilot landed the plane softly, and I was itching to get off. I flipped off airplane mode on my phone, knowing that I was going to have to be in contact with someone. Figure out how to get to the hospital.

If the pilot could taxi a little faster...

Finally, we were pulled to gate. The seatbelt lights were hardly off, and I was unbuckled and standing from my seat, antsy to get off this fucking metal bird.

I needed to get off...

I needed—

My phone pinged, announcing messages, now that my data was turned back on. I glanced at the screen, taking in the quick influx of names:

Trina's parents.

Luc Gagnon, the man who was more a father to me than my own had ever been.

Sam, his son, and therefore, my pseudo-brother.

Molly.

I swallowed hard at seeing Anderson's nanny's name on my screen.

Hell, 'nanny' was just the term we used for her when it came to my accountant.

Molly was Trina's friend.

One of her only friends in the states.

Truly *only* unless you counted the hockey wives and girlfriends she'd gotten to know in the last year.

Trina and Molly met when I was playing in Minnesota, right before Anderson was born. When my wife brought up hiring Molly as a nanny, I was put-off by it. Not because I didn't like the girl, but because we didn't *need* a nanny. Trina was home, and it wasn't like

I was gone *all* of the time. But, when Molly came out for an informal interview, I realized that it wasn't so much a nanny that Trina wanted, but a close friend who was around—and *that* I could support.

I had an entire locker room of guys I could befriend. Trina had no one, *knew* no one, other than me. She was in a new country with a new husband and a new baby…

The least I could do was let her find a girlfriend.

So, at the laughing expense of my wife, I moved money around in our budget, so I would feel comfortable 'affording' her, and contacted our accountant. The next day, Anderson was born.

Molly was as much a part of his life, as Trina and I were.

Because Trina and Molly were damn near connected at the hip, she went up to Quebec with Trina and Anderson for Christmas. I wasn't sure why she didn't go home to her own family, but again, it made Trina happy, so I was for it.

Now, though…

My thumb hovered over Molly's name. She'd tried to get ahold of me the most times, and because of that, I was absolutely terrified of what she was going to say.

All that I'd been told before leaving San Diego, was that Trina and Anderson had been in a car accident, and that I needed to get to Quebec.

Now, I stood, nervous energy coursing through me, as I pleaded in my head for the attendants to open the door. As soon as it was, I was off the plane and rushing through the airport, thankful for my permanent resident card. My messages were the last thing on my mind. I didn't want to see them.

I didn't want confirmation of my fears.

I couldn't…

Fuck. I couldn't live with myself if I knew something bad had happened to either of them.

They're fine. They're fine. They're fine.

In my hand, my cell began to vibrate with an incoming call. As I rushed through the people, I opened the call, not bothering to look at who it was from.

It could only be from Trina's parents, the Gagnons, or Molly.

"Mikey." Molly's voice came out in a whoosh.

My steps faltered, but I pushed on. "How are they? Tell me they're okay, Molly. Tell me…" I swallowed hard, looking to my left, my right, then heading down the left hallway. My dress shoes clicked against the polished floors, slipping in some spots.

"I've got a car in the pick-up line, right outside," she said, avoiding my questions.

"Molly." My blood was roaring through my ears. "Molly, just tell me." The feeling in my gut was horrible. Something was terribly wrong.

Why wasn't she telling me anything?

"We have to get to the hospital," she managed, and I could hear the slightest of cracks in her voice. "Please, just hurry." Then she hung up on me.

Molly hung up on me.

Growling my frustration, I pocketed my phone in my sport jacket and tried to focus on the anger, the unknowing…

But when I got through the sliding doors and the cold winter air hit my face, when Molly's face came to view…

I just knew.

"No." One word. The only word to pass my lips the moment I saw Trina's only friend. Molly's normally young, jovial face—the one that made her look more like fifteen than twenty—was ashen, her eyes puffy, her brown hair falling out of a badly placed ponytail. I stopped in my spot, still easily fifteen feet between us. "No. They're fine. Molly, tell me they're fine." I could not be a twenty-two-year-old widow, who lost both his wife and his son. I couldn't be.

A sob broke from her lips as she lifted a woolen mitten to her mouth, her eyes filling with tears.

"Molly, tell me!"

My feet were glued to the concrete.

I couldn't move if I tried.

For the second time in twelve hours, my world began to move in slow-motion. The sounds of cars moving and loading, planes taking off, people chatting, a solitaire bell being rung outside the small airport…it all faded out. All I saw, all I could fixate on, was Molly's face as her shoulders folded in, tears falling from her eyes, and her head…

Shaking no.

CHAPTER ONE

PRESENT DAY, NOVEMBER 22ND

MIKEY

"Anderson!"

I let the door to the garage slam behind me as I stormed through the house. The one-story ranch was void of any noises—no television, no video games, no mindless chatter that I associated with my son and his nanny—but I knew he was home; Molly's car was in the drive. We didn't live anywhere close enough for them to have walked somewhere, so my kid was here somewhere.

"Anderson!" I yelled again, growing annoyed. First, the kid gets suspended, but then he's not anywhere to be found?

Through the laundry/mud-room, past the living room, kitchen, and down the left hall I stalked, but before I could reach my son's room, the door opened just enough for Molly to slip out, shutting it behind her. She stood there then, her arm wrapped behind her as she held on to the door knob, and her back flush to the jam.

"Don't protect him," I growled, my irritation growing. The very last thing I'd wanted to hear after a late optional-skate was that my son was suspended through Thanksgiving break. I had a game tonight, and then was out of town over the weekend; sure,

Molly would be here, but my son's discipline fell on *me*.

My irritation was no match for Molly though. Hell, it never was. She simply lifted her chin, giving me her own glare.

"You need to calm down." She was the only person I knew who didn't take my bullshit—and it pissed me off.

Molly's and my history was…*rough*.

The only reason why I kept her around, was because Anderson loved her—or so I often tried convincing myself. It had nothing to do with the fact I'd been remembering times when we weren't going head-to-head.

Nothing to do with the fact that these days, I *saw* her.

And that pissed me off even more.

After the accident, I kept Molly on as Anderson's nanny because the contract my lawyer had my wife and I put together for Molly's services was a year-to-year basis, and her year started and ended on Anderson's birthday. With the death of Trina, I could have worked around it, but I'd been a fucking zombie the first few months. Never mind the fact, that while it killed me to admit it, I hadn't been in the right frame of mind to take care of my own kid. Not when he was nineteen-months-old and getting into every godforsaken thing he could reach.

I'd also refused to let my or Trina's families take him, no matter the timeframe. Anderson was my kid, not theirs. He belonged in San Diego with me, not Quebec with either of them.

When Anderson was two, after I finally moved through my grief, and the first time I tried letting Molly go, it took three nannies in two weeks before I succumbed and asked her back. Let her go again when he was five, only to beg her back five days later—after my *kindergartener* damn near got kicked out of school. Then, when he was eight, adult mistakes were made, and it was her decision to leave.

Anderson had missed her.

The house felt empty without her around.

And dammit, I'd missed her too.

A week, then two, passed before I tried calling her, asking her to come back. She wouldn't; said it was better that way. Anderson went through one nanny and eventually, it seemed like my only hope was dropping the kid off at the Prescott house, where he didn't necessarily get along with *their* nanny, but he got along with the boys. I tried convincing myself that all Anderson truly needed was care after school on days I had games, and the occasional overnight trip. I was home; he had school; he had friends. We would be fine without Molly.

She came back after five and a half weeks—the longest she'd been gone—and I learned that her being on my door stoop had nothing to do with me, but due to my son's phone calls. She made *that* abundantly clear

I stopped trying to fire her; my son needed her.

Maybe because she was the only mother-figure he had, but some days…

Fuck, there'd been days that looking at her was a punch to the gut. A reminder of what I'd had, what I'd lost, and what I'd never have again.

And, what I took, and shouldn't still want.

"Mike." Her voice was hard, jerking me away from my thoughts. I clenched down on my jaw. She was the only person on the planet who called me Mike, and she only did it when she was irritated—namely, with me.

Join the club, Molly.

"He's my kid, not yours. Let me talk to him," I forced out, my voice low.

"Not until you calm down," she repeated, her eyes dark and fierce. "He does *not* need you stomping into his room and yelling—"

"He got fucking suspended!" I roared. "For a *fight*. In *fifth grade*! Two days before Thanksgiving! The kid is grounded."

"Yeah, and you don't even know the full story." Her glare went right through me, a piercing brown hold locking me in place.

"Molly. *Move.*" I took a step toward her. Any other person, and they'd have cowered. I was easily a foot taller than her, outweighing her by at least one hundred pounds—and the woman was all muscle from her CrossFit addiction.

But Molly didn't cower.

Not to me, anyway.

She just lifted that stubborn chin of hers, her eyes never wavering from mine.

"Calm down." Her voice was low and eerily even.

Probably why my son listened to her so damn well.

I bunched my jaw and glared up at the ceiling. I wasn't getting anywhere.

"The fight wasn't his fault," she said quietly, the irritation no longer lacing her words, and I dropped my chin to look at her again.

I opened my mouth to refute it, the bubbling anger and irritation right there, but Molly kept going. "He was standing up for a friend."

I scoffed. "He knows better than to throw a punch." When a kid had pseudo-uncles who started shit on the ice, it was important to show him that even if Winski was punching the life out of someone, or Ports was talking shit left and right during a game, the guys were joking and hanging out with the guy from the other team after. Fighting and wrestling and MMA...they were all just entertainment.

Anderson knew better than to fight.

He knew better than—

"He was standing up for Ali." Molly's brows were raised, her mouth tight, as if she was waiting for my comment—a comment she knew I was going to make.

"Ali is a grade younger than him."

Ali O'Gallagher was the youngest daughter of a local pub owner, Conor. O'Gallaghers was the Enforcers' hang out, and Conor and his wife were good friends with Caleb Prescott—once player, now coach. Con's kids hung out with Caleb's, which would be how Anderson knew the girl, but it still didn't explain why the hell my boy was sticking up for her.

Molly shook her head, and rolled her damn eyes, clearly exasperated with me. "You can get the story from him, but don't go in there, guns roaring, Mikey. Anderson's a good kid."

"Pretty sure I know that." Now I sounded like a damn fifth

grader myself. It was in these moments—the ones where Molly was clearly the better parent—that she brought out the worst in me.

It shouldn't be Molly here, but Trina.

Trina should have been the better parent, between me and Anderson's female figure.

If I were being honest though, I was long past Trina-not-Molly thing, and instead, it was just a Molly thing.

You like the girl.

My mind flashed to that morning, not that long ago, when the dynamic between us fully shifted. The morning that everything changed.

A morning that I'd thought about more often than not over the last few weeks.

No fucking business thinking about it.

But, fuck me for wanting it all the same.

"He has a science project to work on tonight, so we won't be going to the game. I'll be back before you have to leave," she said, her arms falling to her sides.

"He can—"

Molly shook her head, cutting me off. "No, he can't go to the game." She always knew what the hell I was going to say. "He's put this project off for a week, and his teacher still expects it to be delivered tomorrow morning."

I frowned at the knowledge Anderson put this project off for so long. Why hadn't Molly—

"I'm his nanny, Mikey," she said, doing that voodoo shit again, cutting off my thoughts with the correct answer. "He's ten. He and I have talked about responsibility and choices. Waiting until the last minute was his choice, and the consequence is, he doesn't go to the game." She shrugged, as if it made all the sense in the world.

Which, truthfully, it did.

Sighing, I shook my head, my irritation dissipating.

"I'll be back in an hour," Molly continued. "I just have to run to the grocery store, but I'll be back in time for you to head to the arena."

When she slipped past me, her back to the wall and her eyes shifting away, I began to reach for her arm, but Molly tightened it closer to her side. Her eyes flashed, jerking to mine for the smallest of seconds, and I stuffed my hand in my pocket instead, watching her walk away. I stood there in the hall of my house, pining after a woman I had no business wanting, but wanting her all the same.

I listened for the front door to open and close again before moving to talk to Anderson. If an outsider were to ask, I'd tell them I stood out here to cool myself down over my son's suspension before talking to him.

When in reality, it was Molly.

This thing with Molly…

The early years, right after I lost Trina, I wanted to hate her. She should have been in the car with them, not sitting at the Perri's house, eating Christmas cookies. Whatever errand Trina had been on, should have been Molly doing.

For the longest time, I resented Molly for being here, when Trina wasn't.

But then…

Then I began to *see* Molly, and it made me feel like a shit person. Molly had been Trina's friend; she was Anderson's nanny. I fucking *employed* her.

Watching her care for my son shouldn't have hit me in the heart the way it did. She was so damn good to him. *For* him.

A shrink would probably tell me I was projecting. Of course, she was good to Anderson; she was paid to be…or so I once tried to convince myself at times—that her care was simply because she was getting a check.

I knew Molly loved Anderson like he was her own, just like I knew she and Trina had been close like sisters. And I knew Molly was a good person. Everyone who met her, loved her. She was easy to get along with—until you did the one thing that could ruin that.

After I started seeing her for who she was, it had helped knowing she'd been in a long-term relationship. It was a shitty thing, to court your wife's best friend; shittier thing when she was your kids nanny.

But then when her relationship ended abruptly…

Yeah. That ended, and then you almost lost her for good that time too. Stop thinking about it.

It was hard *not* to think about it—especially when I knew she distanced herself because of me; because of that day.

These last twenty-three months had been long. I knew she was here for Anderson; I knew it, yet still I wanted things back to what they were *before* that late morning in December. When things were finally easy and comfortable; when I kept my growing attraction to her, firmly locked in a box, not to be looked at.

…But, damn me to hell, I wouldn't take back that morning for all the money in the world and, as much as I told myself *no, never again*…fuck, I wanted it again.

And again.

And maybe again, just for good measure.

What kind of asshole did that make me?

This non-thing with Molly was something that had been weighing on my mind the last few weeks, and the timing to figure it out wasn't ever all that great.

Case in point? I had a suspended fifth grader I needed to talk to. Figuring out this shit with Molly would have to wait.

For now.

But she and I were talking.

Soon.

Without another moment of hesitation, I pushed through Anderson's door.

My son sat on his bed, his knees drawn up, with his arms crossed over his chest, trapped behind his knees. For a moment, I took him in—the freckles on his face, his blonde wavy hair a mess, and the stubborn set to his jaw. He avoided looking at me.

"You want to tell me what this afternoon was about?" I asked, trying to keep any heat from my voice. I was still pissed, but Molly was right—he didn't deserve me to come in here, yelling without the full story.

I was told he'd gotten into a fight on the playground, and that he was being sent home for being the instigator.

Of course, at first, I was angry but dammit, I knew my boy.

Even without Molly's comment that the fight had something to do with a girl, I knew Anderson wouldn't pick a fight for no good reason.

He was a good kid—something else I didn't need Molly telling me, to know it was true.

Anderson grumbled, turning his face further away.

"What happened?" I tried again, crossing my arms and planting my feet shoulder-width apart.

"It's not a big deal," he mumbled.

My brows rose at that. Not a big deal? Kid was suspended, and it wasn't a big deal?

"Yeah, Anderson, it is a big deal. You don't—"

"Pick fights. Yeah. I know." His time with Molly was showing, in the sarcasm of his words. Still, though, his head was turned toward the window.

I probably wasn't helping matters, my arms crossed and brooding, so with a sigh and a prayer to Trina to help me through this, I relaxed and walked toward my son's bed.

"C'mon, Anderson. Talk to me."

When I sat at the end of the bed, he tried turning his head further, shifting his hips so he could. Something wasn't right.

"Look at me, Anderson." Did my boy get hit? Why was he trying so hard not to look at me? I mean, I got puberty and hormones, and knew that it was only a matter of time before I wasn't my kid's best friend, but he'd never *not* talked to me.

He sighed heavily, his entire body moving with it. I watched as he bunched his jaw, his eyes shifting further away. If this was a preview of his teen years… Shit, I'd be in trouble. I didn't know how to do this talk calm and rationally thing—and I rarely had to do it, because Anderson *was* a good kid, didn't get into trouble…but for those few times Molly had left us.

This was what Molly was good at. She and Anderson had probably been talking, and he spoke freely with her. Not like this, when he puts up a giant wall between us.

Finally, Anderson turned his face toward me. His lips were pursed, and the first thing I noticed was, hell, my boy had tears in his green eyes. Then, that he was sporting the beginnings of a nice shiner.

"Shit, Andy," I murmured, using the nickname he grew out of the year before. He hated it but didn't say anything now.

I reached out to cup his chin and turn his face, my thumb gingerly brushing over the lower red swell.

"I didn't throw the first punch." He sounded equal parts worried of my reaction, but proud for standing up for a friend.

I scooted nearer so I could hold his chin with one hand and use my other to gently palpate around the swelling, like I was a damn doctor or something. I wasn't, but I'd nursed a black eye or two in my years.

"I sure as hell hope the other kid was suspended." My anger was beginning to rise again. If that kid didn't get the same punishment as Anderson, shit was going to fly. Oh, let's not forget the fact the school, in their call to me, forgot to mention *my son had a black eye*!

"Dad."

I loosened my jaw, not realizing I had been grinding my molars so hard.

"It's really not a big deal."

"Yeah, Anderson, it is kind of a big deal. Did the nurse look at your face?" I dropped my hands to my lap, my eyes searching his.

Anderson nodded, but didn't elaborate.

Kid knew better than to skirt issues.

"Anderson."

His answering sigh was exaggerated, and I had to fight back a laugh. God, he really did spend a lot of time with Molly.

"She looked, but it was only red then, and no, Isaiah did *not* get suspended but that's because I think I broke his nose. That's why a nose bleeds, right? So, the teachers thought I was the one who was the bad kid even though Ali tried saying it was Isaiah and his friends first." I tried to cut in, but Anderson kept going. "But dad, they were making fun of her! And they knocked her glasses off her face. I mean, I know she sees fine without them, just needs 'em for reading. She just forgot to take them off before lunch. But they knocked 'em right off her face and were pushing her and they were just being mean to her. I wasn't going to let them get away with it." Then, he set his stubborn chin again, his face clearly daring me to tell him what he'd done was wrong.

He did have a point.

"I really wish you hadn't gotten into a fight, but I'm glad you stood up for your friend," I finally answered. "But..." Anderson's face fell a bit. "I'm going to talk to the school and Molly's going to take you into the doctor."

"But—"

"Just to be sure nothing's broken."

He frowned. "Can you break an actual face?"

I barked out a laugh, finding a smile I didn't think was possible after I first got the news. Shaking my head, I said, "God, I love you, kid."

CHAPTER TWO

MOLLY

I sat in my car, idling in the grocery store parking lot, far longer than necessary.

I didn't want to get back to the Leeds's household until absolutely necessary; I couldn't be around Mikey. Ideally, I'd get back right before he had to leave, and not a minute sooner.

The man...*infuriated* me.

But he also confused me. I'd never been so confused with a man, as I was with Mikey Leeds. In all the years I'd known him...

I could remember the first time I met him. It was one of those moments you *couldn't* forget, no matter how hard you tried.

I'd been in a relationship with a decent guy who lived in my apartment building, so it wasn't attraction that I'd felt the day Trina introduced me to her hockey playing boyfriend.

It was awe.

The way Mikey looked at my friend, like she was his entire world...

Thinking of Trina, I leaned over to drop open the glove compartment, and pulled out the card I kept there. Every now and then, I just needed to see her handwriting; to try and hear her voice, even if it was only a fading memory.

Trina had been my family.

My mother passed when I was too young to remember, and while my dad and stepmom had been great growing up, they chose to distance themselves shortly after my eighteenth birthday, for reasons I still didn't know, and likely never would. I met Trina during a particularly dark time in my life, but it was easy to forgo loneliness and despair when you had a bright, bubbly blonde chattering away.

Trina's love for life was infectious, and when she chose to call you 'hers'? You knew her love ran deep. I swallowed hard, running my finger over the swirling ink of her perfect penmanship.

My Molly-Doll:

Sweet girl, I'm so glad you are in my life. Thank you for making my transition to the States easy. Thank you for loving my baby like he is your own. You, lovely, are meant for great things and I cannot wait to watch you achieve them. You are worth more than you think.

You, Molly, are more than my friend; you are my sister, and I love you.

xx, Trina

That had been a hard day, for no particular reason. I'd been single for a few weeks, but I wasn't missing Jack. We parted ways amicably.

But still, I'd been hit with loneliness.

Back then, mostly I felt that I was succeeding at the being-alone-in-the-world thing, but every now and again, the loneliness would hit me, a big one-two punch to the heart.

Watching Trina with Mikey and Anderson.

Sitting at the park with Anderson, watching the other moms and their babies.

Eating at a restaurant with Trina, and seeing the couples, young and old, having a good time.

Everyone happy. Everyone with someone.

It didn't have to be romantic; it wasn't romance I was craving.

It was companionship.

Family.

And while I had Trina's friendship, and I adored the baby who gave me gummy smiles the moment he heard my voice...I'd often felt like an intruder in Trina's life.

That day, I'd thought I kept the sadness to myself, but of course, my friend saw right through me. At the end of my day with her and Anderson, I'd gotten to my car only to find a bouquet of yellow tulips sitting on the driver's seat with this card.

Now, nearly ten years after finding the card, I couldn't always make out the tone of her voice, but I could always *feel* the French tilt of her words. *God, I missed her.*

These days, I still felt like an intruder, only now, I was the one raising her son, making sure her house ran smoothly, that there were groceries in the pantry and fridge.

It may not be the *house* Trina had lived in—Mikey and Anderson moved out of their first house when Anderson was three—but home was rarely a place, but a person, a feeling...and Mikey and Anderson had been Trina's home.

A home I had no business wrecking.

The moment my friendly *like* of the man turned to attraction and want...

I swallowed hard, trying to keep my mind present. I didn't need to remember his hands.

His mouth.

His body...

"Have a good day, Molly," Anderson's first grade teacher said after I signed him in, putting the flower-tipped pen back in the holder.

I smiled, then glanced behind her to where the blond-haired boy I cared for sat in a circle with his classmates. "You guys too. His dad will pick him up today." It was an early release day, and a day Mikey didn't have a game, so after dropping Anderson off for the morning, I was done for the day.

"Sounds good. Oh, wait!" She turned toward a basket, sifting through the papers. "Anderson's dad never brought in his

permission slip for our social this morning. You don't have it, do you?"

I shook my head, "No, I'm sorry. I think I saw it somewhere; I can grab it quickly." The Leeds's only lived ten minutes from the school and while I was Anderson's emergency contact, I wasn't allowed to sign his permission forms.

"Could you? I'd hate for him to have to miss out."

I smiled, shaking my head. "Yeah, it's not a problem at all."

By the time I got to the house, Mikey's car was in the garage. He'd had an away game the night before, and I'd stayed the night with Anderson. When we left for school, Mikey still hadn't been home, so I was a little surprised to see his car there now. When I walked into the house, though, it was silent; no television, no blender.

Huh.

Mikey must have gone straight to bed.

No worries. I could be in and out quickly; he'd never know I'd come back.

The ranch house was designed so Anderson's room, and the one I used whenever I stayed over, were to the left of the living room and kitchen, and Mikey's room was to the right. Even if I were to make noise, he probably wouldn't even notice I was there.

In Anderson's room, I sifted through the folder that was on top of his bookshelf. I tried to keep important papers in it, and every now and then, the wrong ones would end up between the Kraft-brown sides. I knew I'd seen the permission slip somewhere, but as I thumbed through the papers, I realized it wasn't there.

Maybe I saw it on the fridge.

After putting the folder back, I headed toward the center of the house, where the kitchen was. Sure enough, on the fridge behind Anderson's weekly print-out that the teacher sent home every Friday for the following week, was the signed form.

I slipped it off the magnet but when I turned...

From where I stood, and how Mikey's door was hinged, I could see just inside his room, and what I saw had my heart slowing, before racing in an uneven staccato.

The door stood ajar, with perfect view of Mikey's bed.

And it wasn't Mikey sleeping on the bed that caught my attention.

Oh, no.

It was his strong backside, his tight ass, as he knelt behind a woman on all fours, his muscles bunching and moving with each roll of his body, each thrust of his hips.

Good God, the man was magnificent.

And Oh, my God, I can't be seeing this!

My mouth was hanging open, salivating; my heart racing as I watched him fucking a woman from behind. Now that I'd noticed, I could hear the soft grunts, the moans of pleasure coming from both him and her.

Shaken, I swallowed hard and left quickly, vowing to never think of this moment again.

Even now, the memory had me panting.

But then again, now I knew the feel...

I shook my head quickly, then reached for my phone, checking the time.

It would be safe to head to the house now.

The drive wasn't particularly long and, once there, I parked in the same spot I always did, before grabbing the bags containing mine and Anderson's dinner. When I walked into the house, I expected the television on and Mikey ready to head out, but the TV was off, and instead of waiting for me on the couch, Mikey leaned against the kitchen counter, thumbing through his phone.

He was a beautiful man in regular-day attire and even in gym clothes.

He was a walking GQ ad in his pre-game suit. Pressed slacks. Properly sized and tucked dress shirt. And even though he had the sleeves down right now, I could picture them rolled up, showing off his strong, corded forearms.

He looked like he'd been waiting on me to get back but, upon checking the time on the microwave behind him, I saw I was on time.

"Sorry," I still said. "You can head out."

I walked to the opposite side of the kitchen counter, needing space between us, to put the grocery bag down. From inside, I pulled out the box of noodles and the makings of homemade spaghetti sauce.

"I want to talk to you real quick before I head out." His voice was near—far nearer than the space I put between us allowed—and when I looked up, I realized he'd silently walked toward me. My eyes were level with the knot in his navy-blue tie, and I forced myself to look up further, past the already stubbled jaw and to his green eyes.

The same pretty green his son had.

"Yeah. Sorry I took so long," I managed, looking back down at the bag and contents.

Mikey was silent at that—probably taking in my minimal grocery haul and figuring that it didn't take forty-plus minutes to grab these few items.

I grabbed the blue box of noodles and moved toward the other counter, the one that held the stove top, putting space between us once more.

"So, what's up?"

Thankfully, Mikey stayed at the island, where he bunched up the now-empty plastic bag. "One, I called Anderson's pediatrician. If you could bring him into the office at four-thirty, I'd appreciate it. I just want his eye looked at. From what I felt, it's just swollen, but I'd hate for there to be a fracture or something, and we do nothing." Then he shrugged. "Not that there's much we can do for that, but I'll be damned if the school gets away with writing it off as a simple fight when my son was actually hurt."

Mikey's voice had started out calm, but the further into his talk, the more passionate and angry his voice got.

When I'd first met Mikey, he was the laid back, easy to laugh type. Losing Trina brought a very protective side of him out. He was still that laid-back guy, until something pissed him off. And, he was stubborn to a fault.

His son was just like him.

It was no wonder I loved…Anderson.

I swallowed hard, past the guilt of my thoughts, and nodded. "Okay. Yeah, I can do that."

"Two, if you could stick around in the morning, that would be great. I want to go into the school and talk to the nurse who saw him today. Shit, she probably wasn't the nurse, but one of those stand-ins." Again, his voice was bordering that line of calm and angry, but he shook his head and continued on. "Then three…" Mikey took a deep breath, looked away for a full three seconds, before his eyes locked in on mine. "In the next day or so, we're going to have to talk about your job."

My heart fumbled in my chest, and my jaw slackened.

"Like you said, he's ten," Mikey continued, pushing away from the counter. And was I imagining it, or did his eyes do a quick once-over of me? Surely that hadn't just happened.

"But—"

"Four-thirty, Bay office." He said, as if he didn't just essentially pull the rug out from underneath my feet. "Anderson's in his room, working on that project. Thanks, Moll."

And then he was gone.

CHAPTER THREE

MIKEY

Run and evade.

Run and evade, Mikey-boy.

When I told myself earlier that I was going to have to figure out how to talk about...*things*...with Molly, I didn't really figure I'd just blurt it out there.

We're going to have to talk about your job.

Yeah, no shit, she looked worried when you left.

I shook my head; I needed to stop thinking about Molly. At least for now, as I pulled into the apartment complex that Ryan Fitzgerald lived at. Well, the complex the Enforcers organization threw all the new guys.

Fitz was the newest in the locker room.

Twenty-year-old kid from Minnesota.

I figured those Prescotts thought they were pulling a fast-one on me, making me essentially face who I was, once upon a time. Make me pick up and mentor the new kid—the new kid who was, basically, me.

The difference between Fitz and me?

He'd played University of North Dakota for a season.

He never dealt with the political bullshit that came with moving over the border a couple of times.

Nah.

Fitz wasn't me.

"Hey," he said, pulling open the door and slamming himself into the leather seat.

"What's up?" I didn't even give him a chance to buckle or answer; I was pulling my Tesla out of the parking spot and heading for the freeway.

"You in a hurry or something?"

I glanced over and saw Fitz looking at me, amused.

"We have a game."

"Dude, you got to my apartment five minutes early. We've got time."

Looking at the clock, I saw that he was correct. Shit. Things with Molly really threw me off.

"How'd things go with the kid?" Fitz asked, making small talk.

He was a talker. Every damn time I picked him up before a game, talk talk talk talk talk.

I'd have to see if someone else wanted to pick the kid up next week. I needed calm.

Zen.

Quiet.

Before a game.

And, considering I had a son and a nanny at the house, quiet was what I got on the drive to the arena.

The illusion of which was crushed the day Mykaela Prescott-Johnson walked into the room we were going over stats in, looking over all of us players, her eyes eventually landing on me.

"You. Mikey. You're in charge of the new kid."

The Prescotts ran the team unlike any other team I'd been a part of. Okay, so there weren't many on the list of "Who Mikey Leeds played for", but when you worked in this environment, you heard stories, and the stories of a Prescott-run locker room?

They didn't match the rest of the NHL organization.

It wasn't that the buddy-system was a new concept to the hockey locker room. That happened in many cities.

It was simply *how* the Enforcers made that decision.

It wasn't Caleb Prescott, at coach.

It wasn't Trevor Winski, with the 'C' on his chest.

Hell, it wasn't even those of us suited up for the game.

No.

It was the Director of Player Personnel.

Probably because everyone listened when Myke spoke.

Which was why she was great at her job. She was a great liaison for the guys, and not only because she had vast knowledge of the sport thanks to growing up under Prescott rule, but she'd started a pro women's hockey club in the Midwest and knew the vast ins and outs of all aspects to the game.

So, when Mykaela told you that you were going to be the one to walk the new guy through the ropes…

You sighed and did as she asked.

Even if that meant losing the last few minutes of quiet you found.

Snap, snap, snap.

I slapped Fitz's hand out of my view. "Driving."

"How'd it go with the kid? You ran out of the weight room like the devil was on your tail."

"He's fine."

"Wow. Short. Did you ground him?"

"I did not ground him." I was going to ground Fitz though. Into the ground.

Fitz sighed heavily, slouching in his seat. "You on your period today, or what? You're not normally this pissy."

I was supposed to be a role model for the kid, so telling him that he annoyed the shit out of me with his yapping wasn't the correct answer. Instead, I said, "Just juggling things with Anderson."

It wasn't like I kept my kid away from the team. Anderson was at nearly every team family function I was at. He considered the Prescott kids family, and I was glad he had that. But with Anderson, came Molly, and with thoughts of Molly, came my butchering of a speech to her only twenty minutes before.

Thankfully, Fitz stayed quiet then.

For three minutes.

"So, master," Fitz said, crossing his arms over his chest and looking out the passenger window, "and by master, I mean teacher. Tell me. When do you think I should look for permanent digs?"

Giving up on the quiet, I gave in to his questions. "Your contract is what, three years? Five?"

"Five. But burned a year." Meaning, his contract years and entry-level contract shifted due to not playing.

"Do you really want to live in an apartment complex for longer than you have to?" I'm still watching the road but lift a brow all the same. Stupid questions called for stupid answers.

"Alright. So, I go house hunting during summer." He looks out the window, but I'm not stupid—I'm counting in my head for him to continue.

I don't even get to ten.

"Have you done the roommate thing? Maybe I should find a roomie."

I try to keep the annoyance from my voice, keeping the tone even, although it's flat. "I've not done the roommate thing, no."

"I don't think I could live in a big house by myself."

"No one said you had to be in a big house."

"Tyler—" He doesn't have to give the full name for me to know who he's talking about. The kid is something of a legend, with the newer generation of players.

"We do not mention that kid's name."

"Well, I saw his house on YouTube once—"

"If you don't want a two-story brick mansion, don't get a two-story brick mansion. Houses are different in Texas, anyway. That house probably only cost the kid…maybe a mil. Probably just under. You get that house here? You're looking at two mil, minimum."

"Maybe I could live on the beach."

"If you're thinking of Coach's house," it felt odd talking about a friend as 'Coach' but Fitz only knew Caleb as that, so I couldn't very well go all familiar-territory on him, "that's probably out of your range."

"Shit."

I chuckled; couldn't help it. "My first house was a cheap cottage. It was big enough for my wife and me. Wasn't the prettiest, but that was alright."

"You don't talk about her."

And that right there was why.

The guys on the team who'd been around since I came on, they all knew the story. Hell, you could still find the articles online, if you wanted.

"I mean, I know how she died. I researched you," Fitz continued. "But for having this big love for her, for the fact that you can't play the day before Christmas break...I'm just surprised you don't talk about her."

"Well, would you lookee there, we're here," I said instead, pulling the car into the lot and toward the garage door where the veterans were able to park.

Just in time, too, because thoughts of Trina, so close to inappropriate thoughts of Molly...

Fuck.

I needed to figure this shit out with Molly and move on.

She either needed to leave or...

Or, she needed to stay.

⸻

"Hey!"

I heard Kid Prescott's voice over the countless chirps on the ice, the chants in the stands. Glancing around the zone, I found him, and shot the puck off in Porter's—way open—direction before Jordan Byrd slammed me into the boards.

Byrd had been an Enforcer once.

And then he'd been an Enforcer again.

It was during that again that he mended a few bridges he'd burned the first time he came through.

But now, he played for Toronto, and he took his role—as hockey player and, hell, husband, but that was a story for another day—seriously.

"Shit, Byrd," I mumbled as I pushed away from the boards, shaking my head so my helmet fell back into place. Jordan just gave me the finger with his gloved hand and went right back to work.

Looking over the zone, around the ice, I saw that Porter no longer had the puck, and that instead, it had made its way into the possession of Trace Travers, another new guy in the locker room. He was a veteran with nearly ten years under his belt though; I was happy to play first line alongside him.

I moved around the guard of Toronto, trying to find a place to open up for a shot. Travers moved along the ice, doing a spin move around a Toronto player, but never losing possession of the puck.

It was on the open of one of his spins, that Travers did a magic trick—a slapshot that sent the puck right into the net.

Toronto didn't even know what hit them.

As the red light spun and the arena cheered, Toronto's goalie was still patting his chest.

"Dude, it's behind you," I chirped as I went to greet my teammates in an on-ice hug before we all headed toward the bench for the celebratory fist pounding.

Toronto called a timeout—no doubt because there were only two minutes left in a game that they were trailing by two goals—so we rounded our own bench. Caleb pulled out his white board and gave us a new play, before directing a different line out.

No bother.

I could sit for a few seconds.

Plopping down on the bench, I pulled off my glove by trapping my hand between my arm and chest, then reached in front of me for a water bottle, squeezing the lukewarm liquid into my mouth as I slid further down the bench after being nudged to do so.

"Alright, boys!" Caleb yelled over the ice as both D'Amacos and Nash lined up, with Fitz and Lindell in their spots. "Let's head into Thanksgiving on an up note," he said, softer that time, but with a grin on his face and a hard slap to Porter Prescott's back. His kid brother glared over his shoulder and I couldn't help but chuckle, turning my attention back to the ice.

I had two more shifts before the end of the game, and I'd like to say they were exhausting shifts but...

They weren't.

Even when Toronto pulled their goalie, it wasn't bad.

We had a fully healthy, *strong*, team. And with that, came a big lead in conference ranking.

Game over, we all showered and changed. I did a quick interview, but before I could head to my car, Caleb pulled me into his office.

"You're coming to dinner Thursday, right?" Caleb asked, leaning against his desk. He looked to the clock, and I figured he was doing one of two things—timing when he'd be needed for his own post-game interview, or timing how long he had before his wife called. When we were on the road, he'd do video chats with his youngest kids, but being home, and being ten on a school night, I figured that the clock thing was the interview option. "Unless your family's coming to town. But if they're not, Sydney expects you and Anderson there."

"No, no one's coming down. Doesn't make sense, with the break not really being a break."

"Bring Molly."

Now...

Generally speaking, Molly went with Anderson everywhere, and she usually was issued these invitations too, so it shouldn't have hit me the way it did, but it did.

It hit me.

Hard.

"I'm thinking about ending that," I said, mostly because...

Hell, if I knew.

"I mean, Anderson's ten. I can get him to and from school, and nights that there are games, he's usually here anyway. If he's not here, he's at your place. I mean, I'd have to sit down and talk it all out with Sydney, but she never seems to mind him hanging out with Brandon."

"You finally doing something about the Molly thing?" Caleb's grin was all-knowing. Except, no one knew about the one time I took Molly to bed. The time that I regarded as one of the best days of my life, post-Trina.

If only Molly had felt the same.

"No. There's no Molly thing," I denied. How the fuck...?

"You are one of the most honorable guys that I know, Mikey, but you also lie for shit." Caleb was laughing at me. "Invite her to dinner, please. If you don't, Sydney will. Don't make Sydney invite her."

"She probably already did," I murmured under my breath, which only made Caleb laugh again.

"You are probably right about that. Get home to your boy. I'll see you Thursday."

If you thought a game would exhaust Fitz like exhausting a puppy, you would be wrong.

Games only energized the kid.

Didn't matter how hard he played. Didn't matter if he played ten minutes or twenty; the kid was wired before *and* after games.

After games, at least, I wasn't necessarily looking for quiet, so he could yap all that he wanted. Some post-games, we'd head home with music blaring; sometimes we talked the game.

Tonight, was a mix of both.

But the moment he left the car, the moment I was back to solitude, the radio was off and my thoughts, back on.

Both Anderson and Molly would be asleep by the time I got home.

A fact that tore at me.

Molly stopped waiting up after games, after *that* morning. It was like one single day completely changed everything between us, and honestly, it did.

Sex did that.

For the first few years after Trina's accident, Molly would stay up on game nights, then head back to her apartment. For about two years in there, it wasn't her apartment she headed home to, but to a fiancé.

God, I could remember the day that fucker became her fiancé...

I woke up from my nap groggier than when I'd fallen asleep.

I didn't know why I bothered napping; it wasn't like I was going to play tonight.

I'd dress.

I'd go out for pre-game warm-ups.

And sometime between the start of warm-ups, and the buzzer announcing it was time to go back to the locker room, the fear of the day would grip me.

It had been six years.

Six.

Years.

And I still couldn't play on this day.

Coach knew.

He wouldn't even bother putting me on the game day roster.

Didn't matter that I told him yesterday that I'd play today.

He knew me better than that.

Instead, I'd sit in the box, suit and tie on, watching as Caleb and the boys played the game we all loved.

Fuck, if Caleb could play today, I had no reason not to.

It was his first Christmas after losing his daughter to cancer, but fuck if he was letting that stop him.

Nope. That was just me, the fucking guy who was stuck

in some weird limbo on this day, year after year.

I pulled myself out of bed and walked straight to the shower, needing the heat of the water to wake me up. Molly would bring Anderson home in a little bit. On game days, she always picked him up from school, then took him to some activity—trampoline park, skate park, a regular park... Somewhere she could run off his seven-year-old energy before getting him home and giving me time to nap and get ready for my game.

Molly and I worked like a well-oiled machine when it came to the raising of my son.

My chest ached at that, and at the reminder of the day.

It should have been Trina and me, not the nanny and me.

Somewhere over the last few weeks though, it started to get easier.

It was the sixth Christmas without my wife.

Looking at the tree that Molly put up, didn't hurt so much this year.

Other things this year...Anderson's sixth birthday without Trina here.

Looking at the pictures Molly took of Anderson blowing out his candles, didn't hurt so much now.

The hurt was starting to scatter.

And I didn't think it had anything to do with the fact I was starting to allow myself to find pleasure in other women's bodies...

But rather, in the comfort I found in Molly.

Seven years, I knew the girl.

The first year, I thought she was great. Trina loved her.

Anderson loved her more.

The next few years, I hated her.

But still, Anderson loved her.

And somewhere over the last few weeks...

I saw her.

I saw more than the woman Trina had befriended when we lived in Minnesota. I no longer saw Trina's friend. I didn't see Anderson's nanny.

I saw the too-wide smile on her face, the one that caused laugh lines around her eyes—that was how hard she smiled when she was happy.

The smile that caused two long, deep dimples to appear in her cheeks; dimples that you only saw when she smiled.

I saw the amber glow in the brown depths of her eyes.

The way she twisted her ponytail around her hand when she was focusing on homework with Anderson.

The way she'd pinch his sides when he was acting sour, causing my boy to giggle like the little boy he was starting to lose.

I started to see Molly as a woman I didn't want to employ but wanted to keep around for my own selfish purposes.

And I couldn't very well be signing her paycheck, and then taking her to bed. That was wrong on so many levels.

The problem with letting her go and finding a new nanny, was that I trialed nannies with Anderson, and he was an absolute terror for them. It was probably wrong of me, enabling Anderson and his terrors, by allowing him to dictate who would care for him when I wasn't around, but ultimately, I had to do what was best for my son.

Even if that meant putting my own desires on hold.

Besides, she was in a relationship; a relationship that was something like ten or so months old now.

One that, selfishly, I hoped wouldn't last much longer.

Listen to me, *I thought, pushing my head under the stream of water*, Such a selfish dick.

And I was.

I didn't bring women to the house—not usually, anyway—but I wasn't exactly celibate.

So, I could have sex, but I didn't want Molly having sex, was basically what it came down to.

I wanted her.

And I wanted her badly.

I no longer felt bad about that. No longer hated myself for wanting the single person I once blamed for Trina's death.

Wrongly.

I wrongly blamed her, I knew that now.

Hell, I knew it then.

But I'd needed someone to lash out at, and Molly was there.

Yet, here she still was. Living in my house part time, caring for my son.

Loving my son.

My cock started to stir then, the blood moving south.

The more I thought about Molly, the harder I got.

So hard, that I had no choice but to take my cock in hand and pump myself—because this was an ache that a cold shower wasn't going to fix.

The only fix—and I knew from weeks of attempting otherwise—was to picture her pretty face, her small hands, her long hair...

Then, imagining the feel of her wet pussy.

I squeezed my eyes shut as I leaned forward, resting my head against my forearm as I held it to the tiled wall, pumping myself harder, faster, trying to merge in my mind, moans of women in the past with the voice of Molly. Tried imagining her voice in the throes of pleasure.

After I was spent, I cleaned up the shower walls and finished my shower, the entire time berating myself. Molly was off-limits.

And she always would be.

Something that was further made clear when I walked into the kitchen, dressed for pre-game.

Anderson was sitting at the counter, working on homework and Molly was damn near bouncing around the room as she cooked dinner for the two of them.

"Did you take all of Anderson's energy?" I tried joking, moving past her so I could grab a premade protein shake from the fridge. Before she could answer, I walked over to Anderson and ruffled his hair, pressing a kiss to the top of his head. He dipped away, but I saw the smile on his face.

"Whatcha got, boy-o?" I asked, looking over his shoulder. "Math?"

He nodded but kept working. I ruffled his hair again, and looked back to Molly, who was still smiling as she cooked pasta for her and Anderson.

"You got plans for Christmas?" I tried. "Heading home?" She never went back to Minnesota. She also hadn't done Christmas with Anderson and me since the accident.

I honestly couldn't tell you what she did during the four-day break.

"Just hanging out with Curtis and his family," she answered, not turning around.

But, at the mention of her boyfriend's name, her smile widened.

I could see her dimples and fuck Curtis for putting them there.

Look at me.

All jealous and shit.

I shook my head of that, cracking open the top of my shake. I chugged it down in two breaths—needed to, because sometimes this shit was nasty.

"Just tell him already," Anderson groaned, not looking up from his homework.

So, whatever had Molly dancing, Anderson knew.

"Tell me what?" I tossed my now empty bottle into the Simple Human garbage can, on the recycling side. "I've gotta go; speak now or hold your peace."

"Hold your pee," Anderson giggled behind me. "Get it. You gotta go?" Then, he giggled again.

Molly whipped around quickly, her hair a fan swirling from her front, over her shoulder, to her back, as she fixed her pretty smile on me.

"Curtis asked me to marry him!"

And then she was shoving her hand under my face, like I gave a damn.

But I didn't.

I didn't give a good goddamn, because it was a fucking kick in the gut.

And it was yet another reason to fucking hate this day.

I pushed the memory back as I pulled into the drive. All the lights were off, as I expected them to be—even if part of me still selfishly wished Molly would stay up.

I wanted someone to talk to.

What was the point of having someone living in your house, if you couldn't find companionship in them?

I walked into the house, locking it up tight. I glanced to my left, to the hallway I knew both Anderson and Molly were. It wasn't the first time that I battled waking her up.

For nothing more than that talk I wanted so badly.

No, not the talk about ending her employment, but just to *talk.*

Talk about the day.

Talk about Anderson's day.

Talk about the appointment I had her take him to.

I could use that as an excuse, I thought. I could wake her up and ask her…

But if it had been something important, there wasn't a doubt in my mind that she'd have called or texted me. She'd have let me know if something was fractured.

And because she didn't, Anderson must be fine.

So, instead of going to her room and waking her to talk, I made myself turn my back on their hall, and head to my own bedroom. It would be enough, the distance.

It would have to be.

CHAPTER FOUR

MOLLY

Usually on mornings after games, I was up by six—enough time to get breakfast and lunch together for Anderson for the school day, and still allow me to slip out before the boys woke up.

It was simply part of the schedule Mikey and I made.

It was also an evasion tactic on my part.

I wasn't going to be able to ignore Mikey this morning, though, and even though Anderson wasn't going to school, I was still up and moving around the kitchen, my regular routine in place.

I'd even already packed my overnight bag; I was ready to head out whenever Mikey got back home from the school.

As much as I wanted to hang out with Anderson, I really didn't want to hang out with Mikey, so the sooner he got up, moving, to the school and back, the better for my psyche.

I was sitting at the counter, mindlessly eating a toasted bagel with peanut butter when Mikey finally came out of his room.

Finally. I mentally laughed at the sarcasm. As if six-thirty was incredibly late in the day.

I looked over my shoulder at him and offered him a smile—tight because of the peanut butter, not the lingering fears and wants.

"You got another one of those?" he asked, scratching his

chest over the worn blue t-shirt he wore.

I swallowed what was in my mouth. "Bagel?"

He nodded as he walked to the coffee maker, pouring into one of the white mugs he had hanging above it.

"There's another in the fridge. Another bag in the freezer." I took another bite of my breakfast, hoping to stop the conversation.

The small talk.

Mikey and I hadn't done true small talk in so long, I didn't really know how to go about it anymore.

He turned then, his butt resting against the counter and his legs crossed in front of him. He wore loose pajama bottoms and for the briefest of moments, I wondered if he wore anything underneath…

I could feel my blush to my toes, so I looked down at what remained of my peanut butter bagel and stuffed it into my mouth.

"Anderson can sleep in," Mikey said after a few moments, putting his coffee mug beside him on the counter after no doubt, drinking at least half.

How did I figure?

He got chatty.

That could only mean that he had caffeine in his system.

"Before he wakes up and before I head to the school—"

"I put his project in your car. You can drop it off when you head in."

"Will do. I thought we could—"

I interrupted again. "I know these are special circumstances, but I need you to be back by nine-thirty. I have an appointment."

"Can I talk?"

I sighed heavily and looked down to my now empty plate. I didn't want to talk.

I didn't want to lose my job.

Lose the last piece of normalcy that I had.

For years, my life revolved around Anderson Leeds.

What was I going to do without taking care of him?

I could only go to my CrossFit gym so many times a week, and sometimes, that tenth session in a seven-day period was killer on your body.

I could go to school.

Before meeting Trina, I'd considered being an early elementary teacher.

"Moll."

I looked up and over the counter at him. There he was, looking cool, calm, and collected in sleep pants, a t-shirt that stretched over his chest just so, and messy bed head.

Oh, let's not forget the dark stubble on his cheeks.

Maybe it actually was best to step away now.

Being here...having these thoughts and feelings...

"You're right," I said, still not letting him talk. I didn't want to hear it from his mouth. It was easier to be the one making the decision. "I mean, not that you've said it, but I get the feeling that the talk is about the fact I pointed out that Anderson is ten and probably doesn't really need full-time a nanny anymore. I gotta be honest, I'll miss him like hell but—"

"Molly. Damn woman, let me talk." Was that a half grin on his face?

He thought this was funny?

I clenched my jaw tight and slipped off the stool, taking my plate to the sink.

"Yeah, Molly," he started, and I could feel his eyes on my back. "You're right. He's probably getting too old for a constant caregiver, and I *am* home most of his day. You've been great help over the years and we both know that Anderson does really well with you. I don't want you to leave his life."

I turned off the water to the sink and hung my head. "Oh." I took my moment to try and calm myself, then turned to the dishwasher, drying my hands on the towel that was there.

"I was curious though," he started, but the tell-tale sign of a door opening stopped whatever it was he wanted to say.

"Morning," Anderson announced, walking down the short hall and into the kitchen, his feet shuffling along the tiled floors.

I forced a smile on my face as I turned. "Morning, sleepy." He came to me first, for a morning hug. A fact I was sure that Mikey didn't miss.

When Anderson walked to his father, Mikey ruffled his hair before hugging him back. "Morning, kid. What'd the doctor tell you?"

And suddenly, I felt terrible for not reporting on that. Last night, it hadn't been important enough to text him—Mikey had this fear, and it wasn't irrational, whenever he received texts or calls during games. I didn't want to add that stress to his life, not when it wasn't time sensitive.

"Sorry, Mikey," I mumbled, but it might have been missed, with Anderson talking over me.

"It's fine," Anderson continued on. "Not broken. But it's kinda cool looking today, isn't it?"

Mikey chuckled and shook his head. "Sure thing, bud. We almost had matching shiners. I got into some words with a player last night."

Anderson smiled wide, a smile that was near-identical to his father's. "That would have been cool."

"You two already look too much alike," I butt in, which only made Anderson smile that mini-me smile even wider. "Your dad is going to go into the school to talk to the nurse this morning."

"And principal," Mikey added.

"And principal. Is there anything you need to say or add before he does? Anything you left out in your story yesterday?" I didn't think there was, but now was a good time for him to get it off his chest, if there were additional details.

Anderson shook his head. "Nope. Isaiah and his friends were teasing Ali, and they pushed her. So, I pushed back."

He said it so matter-of-factly, so strongly…

He was headstrong, just like his father.

I often wondered…if Anderson had Trina in his life, what qualities of hers would he have taken on, instead of being a little Mikey Leeds?

"Well, I better change so I can go and get back," Mikey said. "Molly has an appointment."

Anderson nodded. "Hair," he offered with a shrug and a

disapproving shake. "She's gonna cut it all off, she said."

"Anderson." My face probably looked bewildered.

Mikey looked at me then, lifting his brows. "Why?"

I shrugged, wishing Anderson hadn't said anything but it was said so... "Just need a change. Donate it, maybe. Good cause, you know?" That, and I only got my hair done once or twice a year—much to my hairdresser's distaste, of course. But I kept it healthy, even when I threw it in messy buns all the time. Why cut it so often if you didn't need to? And it had been easily sixteen months since I cut it last. It nearly grazed my butt when wet. It was time for it to go.

It needed to be done.

Good thing I didn't mention my doctor's appointment to Anderson. Just what I would need—Anderson airing that too.

After Mikey and I...had our moment that one morning...I tried like hell to keep my personal life very separate from my work life. And, for nearly two years, I succeeded. Or, at least, I thought I did.

At any rate...

I helped Anderson get breakfast together and, not much later, Mikey left for the school.

"What are you going to do the rest of the week, other than that sumo-bar lifting stuff you do?" Anderson asked as he shoveled scrambled eggs into his mouth.

"Ask after you've chewed, Anderson," I warned with a smile, but then continued to answer him anyway. "I don't know. Laundry. Sleep. Maybe go grocery shopping. The weekend will come too fast."

Anderson nodded, scooping another forkful of eggs. Before he put them in his mouth though, he asked his question, "Dad's out of town this weekend, right? Saturday and Sunday?"

"Yeppers."

"Cool. Maybe we can go see that new Marvel movie."

I laughed. "You're supposed to be grounded."

Anderson lifted his brows, his forehead a wrinkled mess, as he shook his head and chewed quickly.

"Don't choke."

He swallowed hard before holding his fork in the air. "It wasn't my fault. I think my sentence should be lessened."

"That's up to your dad, bud."

"I think he'll let me free." He nodded a few times. "Yeah. I think after he talks to them, he'll come around."

"What, you don't want to hang around the house with me? We've gotta go out and do something, for you to be happy?"

"Nah." Anderson's grin was infectious. "You're fun. I just thought maybe going out would be fun too."

"We'll see."

"That means, whether dad ungrounds me or not, we're gonna go out."

My laugh was quick—startling, almost. "I said we'll see. And that means, we'll see."

Nothing flew by Anderson though.

And his continuous smile was the proof. "Yeah. Right. We'll see."

CHAPTER FIVE

MOLLY

Turned out, I wasn't going to have all that much time off, after all.

Not only did Mikey issue an invitation to the Prescott's for Thanksgiving dinner, Sydney Prescott, herself, did too. If it were just Mikey, I probably would have found a reason to say no.

But you didn't say no to the super pregnant wife of the team's coach.

And definitely not at a time when the family was going through so much. The Prescotts' mom wasn't doing so well, with a cancer she wasn't beating.

That family and cancer...

Now, here I sat, playing on the floor with Asher Prescott and her adorable twin girls, Peyton and Presley. They were seventeen-months old, and just about the most fun babies in the universe.

Each had her own personality—Presley, stubborn; Peyton, sweet. And if you didn't know them, they could pass as identical, but when you actually looked at the two of them, you could see there were differences, such as different chins and noses.

"Up, up, up," I said through a smile, lifting Peyton to "fly" over my head. She giggled, and I managed to dodge drool in the nick of time.

"How are things at the Leeds's house?" Asher asked, her eyes on her other daughter.

Asher may have been a few years younger than me, but you could tell from looking at the girl, that her life made her older than her years. Her husband, Caleb's youngest brother, only recently started playing in San Diego, but over the twenty-or-so months that I'd known her, I watched her become a more open person.

"They're going," I said, flipping Peyton so she sat in the hole my crossed legs made. I held a soft book in front of her, and she began flipping through the pages. "I think I might be let go soon, though," I admitted out loud, for the first time.

"No."

I looked up at Asher's voice, seeing the frown on her face.

"He wouldn't."

I shrugged. "He said we had to talk. And we started the conversation yesterday morning, but then Anderson woke up and it wasn't the right time. I mean, I get it. He's ten." I looked down at the top of Peyton's brown-haired head, reaching up to twist the waterspout pony in my finger.

It was a running joke throughout the season that Jonny, the other Prescott, couldn't tell the girls apart. Even though Porter got a kick out of it, Asher tried to make it easy by doing something different with the girls—such as today, Peyton had a ponytail at the top of her head, and Presley had folded pigtails.

I had a feeling that Peyton's was the folded top-knot style at one point too, but her hair was finer than her sister's.

"Who am I going to talk to at the games, if you're not there?"

It wasn't a joke, either. Asher and I had found a friendship over the time they'd been in San Diego; the last few months, especially. It wasn't that she didn't get along with the other wives; it was more that she was much younger than everyone else.

"Hey, maybe Fitz will start bringing a girl," I tried saying, a forced smile on my face. "He's not that much younger than you and Porter."

"Except his maturity level," Asher scoffed, and I couldn't help but laugh.

"Yeah. There *is* that." I shook my head, smiling, as I looked back down at the book Peyton was flipping through once again. I picked up another and held it out, but Peyton pushed it away, content with the one she had.

"Well, damn." Asher sighed, then said, "I wish he would have done it a year ago! We would have hired you."

Now, my smile wasn't forced, but paired with a laugh. "Oh, come on. You love Emersyn."

Asher made a face. "Yeah. She's good."

Still laughing lightly, I shrugged. "Maybe it will just be time for me to go back to school. Finish the degree I never really started. You know, I met Trina right before I started college. And then, the rest, they say—"

"Is history," Asher completed with a thoughtful nod. "What would you go for?"

"Early elementary. Pre-k and kindergarten." It came out of my mouth so quickly, I didn't even have time to think about it.

"You sound like it's something you want."

"Honestly, I'd never really thought about it, not until Mikey first mentioned we needed to 'talk'," I said, lifting one hand in the air to make air quotes. I glanced around the living area to be sure he wasn't around to overhear.

Nope.

He was hanging out in the kitchen with Porter and Eric Christensen, popping olives in his mouth.

"You would be good at it. Heck, I'd beg the school to put the girls in your classroom."

"You think they'd listen?"

Asher nods. "Porter can be persuasive when he needs to be. And for the girls? He'd do it. He listens to my demands."

"You're a hoot," I said around another laugh.

I was glad I came.

When I wasn't with Anderson, I was hanging out at my apartment by myself. It wasn't often that I did the whole girl-time thing, and usually, the only time I saw Asher was during a team function. "We should do this when it's not attached to the team. You know, when I'm not invited anymore." I tried really hard to make that last bit a joke, but I didn't think it worked.

"You'll always be invited, Molly. But yes. I'd like that."

"Does Emersyn ever watch the girls alone? Or does she just do mother's helper things?"

"No, she watches the girls if I have to run to the store or something. She's great with them. I just have nothing to do during the day, and Porter feels better having another set of hands in the house when he's gone. It's not nearly as bad as when the girls were baby-babies, but it's been her schedule for the last year. Why change it, ya know?"

I started to say that I understood that—especially from the nanny point of view—but Caleb clapped his hands loudly in the spot of the open floorplan that allowed everyone to see him. With the noise, the big kids—Caleb's boys and Anderson—came out of the playroom, and the younger ones—Braelyn Prescott and Dylan Winski—turned to kneel on the couch, looking back at Caleb.

"Dinner is ready," he announced. "I slaved over the turkey, so my wife would not have to. I expect you all to eat."

Brandon, every bit his father at ten, clapped his hands too. "Just don't eat the pie. Who knows which one ended up on the floor."

The room erupted in laughter, but Caleb was quick to point out that the pie that fell was in the garbage.

I stayed close to Asher and the girls, even when Porter took Peyton from my arms, blowing raspberries on his daughter's covered tummy. Briefly, I searched the room for Mikey—and caught him staring back.

I looked down quickly, but all was forgotten—forcibly forgotten—when Anderson wedged himself in line in front of me.

"What, you want the best plate?" I joked with him, putting my hands on his shoulders and shaking him from side to side.

"I always get the better turkey, you know that," he joked right back, and it was true.

For years, I was the one making his plate.

Don't get me wrong, Mikey did a lot with Anderson.

But this had always been my role.

And it wouldn't be for much longer.

With that thought in mind, I let it be, giving Anderson a quick hug then pushing him forward as the line began to move.

CHAPTER SIX

MIKEY

I never got to finish that talk with Molly.

She'd driven herself to Thanksgiving and left before Anderson and I were ready to head out.

She came back to the house that Saturday morning, right before I had to leave for the teams' weekend trip.

As in, *right* before I had to leave.

My car was running and everything.

She apologized profusely, but also refused to look me in the eye.

If only I could find an eloquent way to tell her I wasn't considering letting her go for performance sake, but because I wanted to explore other sides of, well...us.

Not that that sounded any better.

In fact, that almost sounded like work-place harassment.

Then, on Sunday when I got home, it was to a voicemail—*I brought Anderson to the Prescotts. Brandon wanted to play pick-up hockey. I figured you'd be home soon, and Sydney was okay with him playing for a bit. See you Tuesday after school.*

Only, by 'see you' she meant, once again, in a brief pass-by.

An entire week of this barely seeing her, hardly passing off my kid...

And I was…

Irritated.

That was the only good word for it.

Fucking irritated.

Leave it alone, Mikey. Just leave it alone.

I should.

I damn well should just leave it alone.

Just because I'd been taking walks down memory lane the last few weeks—hell, months—didn't mean she was.

Just because I was aching for the loss of familiarity we had *before* I slept with her, didn't mean she was. Hell, maybe she had a new boyfriend! Maybe that was why she'd been increasingly distant.

Molly was a grown-ass woman. She certainly wasn't running away from me because I told her we needed to talk.

But hey, maybe she would rather a formal email.

I wasn't sure how well that would go down though:

To Miss Molly Attwood,

I hope you're doing well. I am writing to you in re: to your employment in the Leeds's household. Your services will no longer be needed, not due to your performance, but due to the blood flow in your boss's nether regions.

Frankly, he wants to fuck you.

Signed, Michael Austin Leeds

Yeah.

That'd go over *real* well.

In the end, I was better off just letting her go.

Right?

I couldn't sleep with her when I was paying her.

And hell, she probably didn't want to sleep with me, regardless.

So, I should let her go and try to move on.

Because to be honest?

I hadn't taken a woman to bed in over twenty-three months.

And the last one?

A certain brunette with amber eyes, hidden dimples, and

laugh lines when she smiled.

Fuuuuck.

Me.

But c'mon!

How was I supposed to find a woman—a puck bunny, really, at this point—when I knew what was standing in my house damn near five days a week?

There was also that little fact that I wasn't banking on a relationship with anyone else.

I'd had that.

I lost it.

Been there, done that, didn't care to go through it again.

So, being so caught up in Molly Attwood was as strange as the fact I couldn't find some easy woman to bed for one night. Why she had the hold over me…

You want her, and you want to keep her. You'd break your rules for her.

Yeah.

…Something like that.

Frustrated with my train of thoughts, I dragged my hand down over my face as I sat in the locker room, pants and skates on, but only dressed otherwise in my Nike undershirt. The guys all joked and laughed around me; the atmosphere in the room was due to the game starting off strong.

We were between second and third periods and were up by four goals. Charleston didn't have a hope in winning, not with the way we were playing tonight. Caleb would allow the guys to have fun now, but two or so minutes before we left for the ice again, he'd rein us back in.

It's what he was good at.

While all the guys talked and joked, I sat—alone with my thoughts—thinking about the woman who was up in the family box with my son. The very one I basically had to beg to bring Anderson back home afterward.

"If it's okay with you, Sydney said—" Molly started, as I walked into the kitchen, tying my tie.

"Actually, I wanted to talk to you about Christmas, the holidays. So, if you could stick around for the game..." I pulled the tail through and adjusted the knot, my eyes not leaving Molly as she stood in the pantry door, a can of corn in her hands.

She always had something in her hands.

Was always messing with something.

Needing something to do.

"Oh." She actually *looked disappointed, switching the Green Giant can to her other hand.*

"Thanks, Moll. I appreciate it." I didn't give her a chance to say anything more, by walking down the hall to tell Anderson goodbye.

And while I did want to talk to her about the upcoming holiday—it was only nineteen days away, where the hell had the time gone—I also just wanted to talk to *her*. Figure this shit out and be done with it.

It wasn't affecting my playing game yet, but the fact that all I could think about when I *wasn't* playing was her and us and then and tomorrow...

It needed to be talked about.

Finally, Caleb came back into the room, doing the clapping thing he did, and pulled everyone's attention back to now, to the game. While he talked, and then gave the floor to Winski for a quick pep talk, I pulled my shoulder and chest pads on, followed by my jersey.

It was game time.

Which also meant, thoughts of Molly were put to the back burner.

Thankfully.

For now.

We were doing what we'd been doing best this entire game—giving Jonny extra coverage.

Standing in front of him, the guy most protecting the man, was Winski. Then, there was me in front of Winski, guarding the center pathway, with Kid Prescott playing left, and Easton Nash guarding the men on the other side.

And Fitz, the other D-man on our line?

Oh, he was in the penalty box.

But the four of us out here were a killer PK group. We could take the man-disadvantage and twist it to be a good thing.

Nash was our flex player; he was on the roster as a forward, but had played defense prior to camp, so he rounded out our current group well.

Our penalty kill percentage was top of the league.

We had this.

Charleston played with the puck, around and around the zone, wasting time. Normally when we needed a penalty kill and we were playing Charleston, Nico—not Nash—was on the ice with us, but he'd just played a hard shift.

Nico and Porter knew this team in and out.

They knew their man-up plays, regardless of any roster changes the team had seen over the last year.

Sometimes it was nice having more than one guy on the ice who had playing history with your opponent.

As it was...

We were still killing it.

Charleston's MacDonald looked like he was itching to make a shot, so my eyes were on him, even if the puck wasn't in front of him. The man had tells, worse than a poker player, and I was more than capable of reading them.

Rookie mistake, man.

Sure enough, the puck was slapped across the zone, passing both myself and Winski, and MacDonald lifted his stick, getting ready to meet the puck with a slapshot reply.

I released my stick with one hand, reaching up to try and stop the flying rubber with my glove, but instead of knocking it down, the puck grazed my gloved hand.

Fuck.

Quickly, I turned, the sounds of Charleston yelling, skates scraping ice, fans cheering—or jeering, really—masking out the next few milliseconds.

When you're on the ice, milliseconds sometimes feel like minutes, and that's what this situation felt like.

I watched as the puck that just grazed my glove headed toward Winski, who pulled his body together tight—a human shield. His legs together, arms tight to his body. The way the puck deflected from my glove should have slowed down momentum.

It should have altered the angle.

And it did.

But rather than break the trajectory from a straight path to downward, it caused it to go in an upward arc.

Winski didn't have a chance in hell.

The moment the puck hit his helmet, my stomach clenched.

The moment Winski went down to his hands and knees, I didn't give a damn where the puck ended up.

The next milliseconds flew by.

Cheering from the fans.

Whistle from the refs—with half a mind, I registered that Jonny stopped the puck.

A linesman yelling and waving for San Diego's medical trainer, Trent Mulligan.

The guys and I skated near a downed Winski, who was now slowly pushing his skates back to lay on the ice. Once flat, he rocked his skates side to side, out and in.

At least he was moving.

It was moments like this that the arena was eerily silent.

Everyone holding their breath. Waiting to see what would happen.

To see if number 32 would get up and off the ice on his own, or if he'd need help.

The puck had hit Winski in the helmet, hard enough to send him to the ice; he'd be pulled for concussion precautions, at minimum.

But he was moving. That was good.

He'd be okay.

If I kept thinking it, I'd convince myself it to be true.

Two minutes later, with Trent on one side and me on his

other, we helped Winski back toward the bench, where he and Trent took the tunnel to medical.

Caleb watched Winski walk down the tunnel, then glanced up to the family box. Just one look, and you could feel the history of friendship between the two—it was more than just a coach watching his player.

It was a friend watching, then looking up to where the wives and kids were.

Where Winski's very pregnant wife was.

"He'll be good," I said, not knowing if Caleb heard me.

But then he nodded, glancing back at the bench. "Alright, boys. Let's finish this game."

Molly and Anderson got home before I did, which wasn't unusual. I also knew she'd have had him go to bed already, because he had school in the morning.

Which was good.

After Caleb got an update from Sydney, who got an update from Callie, Trevor's wife, the team was a little down—even though we won the game.

Regardless.

I felt like shit.

The puck deflected from my glove.

It should have slowed down.

Instead, it whacked my teammate—my fucking friend—hard enough to have him blackout moments after leaving the tunnel. He was going to be on concussion protocol for at least the next week, and we had a fairly aggressive schedule coming up.

I walked into my house, dropping my suit jacket and tie onto the top of the washing machine as I stepped through the mud room, not even fully registering the sounds of both the washer and dryer running.

Molly was so damn good at keeping the house moving, going, running.

The moment I cleared the mud room, I saw her sitting on the

couch, crossed legged as her gaze fixed on the television. She still wore the black leggings she'd had on earlier, but instead of the long blouse she'd paired it with for the game, she was now in a sweatshirt that swallowed her whole. One that I'd seen countless times before, when she'd stay the night with Anderson and I was out of town, or home late.

I was hit with the familiarity.

With the knowledge that if she left...

Hell, Molly was the only constant in mine and Anderson's lives over the last nine years.

Molly didn't glance at me as I stepped into the room, but still leaned forward to grab the remote from the table, aiming it at the large entertainment center, and shut the television off.

Even with the sounds hardly registered when I walked in, it was obviously silent now.

"Thanks for sticking around," I said, breaking that quiet. I kept walking past the couch, stopping at the kitchen counter and leaning forward as I toed off my dress shoes. "He get to bed okay?"

"He did. No fight." Her voice was still behind me and if I had to guess, she was still on the couch; probably still facing the television rather than turning to angle back at me.

In my socks, I walked to the fridge and reached for a water...

And instead, pulled out a beer.

I didn't drink after games, not when we had practice in the morning.

I stopped hanging out at O'Gallaghers with the guys years ago—for no reason other than I wasn't a big drinker and had a kid at home.

But I needed the smooth barley and malt right now.

With the cold bottle in hand, I closed the fridge and grabbed the dish towel hanging on the nearby oven. As I twisted off the cap, using the towel as extra leverage, I turned so I was facing the living area.

Facing Molly.

The bottle cap dropped to the marble countertop with a rounding clink, and as I brought the bottle up to my lips, I watched

Molly unfold herself from the couch, turning toward me.

"If you're good—" she started but I shook my head, bottle to my lips. I took a healthy drink from the bottle, then placed it down softly on the counter.

"Sit down, Moll," I finally said, wiping at my mouth with the back of my hand. Leaving the bottle in the kitchen, I walked toward her.

I gave her space though, moving to sit at the other end of the L-shaped sectional.

Before I could figure out how to word this conversation, Molly sighed, bringing her legs back up on the couch to fold at her side. "I understand why you think it's a good time to lose the nanny. But you think maybe it could wait for after the holidays? It's a lot. I mean, not for me." Her brows her up and she placed her hand on her chest. "But for Anderson. You're different around the holidays, Mikey, understandably so, but I don't think it's fair to make it harder on Anderson. Not so close to them anyway."

I opened my mouth to set her straight…

And realized I couldn't.

I physically could not tell her that I wanted her.

It was like a vise gripping my throat; the words wouldn't come out.

"But after the holidays…" She shrugged, her gaze fixed on the coffee table in front of her. Her hair was free of any confines and as such, draped over her far shoulder. Molly reached behind her with her right hand, grabbing for stray strands from her left shoulder, and brought them to the rest of her mass of brown hair. "I get it." She looked over at me and shrugged again, just one shoulder this time. "I do. Besides, I was talking with Asher—"

"They have a nanny." It came out quick. Reflexive.

Shit, I didn't want someone else hiring her.

She was looking already? Fuck.

"I was talking with Asher," Molly repeated, a bit slower with her brows drawn up—not at all unlike an adult scolding a child for interrupting, "about maybe finishing school. I never did. I met you and Tr—" She averted her eyes again, swallowing hard.

"Right." I nodded, knowing where she was going with that.

"So, it's honestly okay," she continued, still avoiding my eyes. She picked at the black stretchy material at her knees and I found myself watching the small movements.

If she went to school, it would mean she wasn't nannying.

Would she finish school back in Minnesota? Or would she stay here?

I wasn't ready to lose her yet, and certainly not half a country away. "Where have you looked?"

She frowned, looking at me again. "Why?"

I shrugged. "Just curious. You're not…" I took a breath and went with it. "You're not moving back to Minnesota, are you?"

"Ha." Her laugh was unamused, even if her eyes danced a little. "There's nothing in Minnesota but cold winters. I like San Diego."

Nothing in Minnesota…?

"Wouldn't your family want you to go home?" I asked, knowing fully well I was fishing for information.

The woman got half of her summers off when Anderson and I spent the month of July in Quebec.

She got Christmas break off, whether Anderson and I traveled to Canada for the holiday or not.

What was she doing during those times, if not going back home?

Molly just shook her head, and I knew she was going to deflect. "The semester starts mid-January. So, if we could figure something out by then, that'd be great. I have friends here and even if I'm not watching him, maybe you'd allow me to take him to games or movies or something."

I was frowning, trying to piece things together, but nodded all the same. "Yeah. Of course. He'd like that." I would too. Why couldn't I tell her that?

Then Molly was standing again, and I had to jump into action. Standing too, I reached for her arm. Unlike the other day, my hand made contact and I swallowed hard at the jolt that went through me.

"Will you go Christmas shopping with me? I was planning on going tomorrow. We don't have a game and Cael's giving us the day. I think he wants to check in on Winski, to tell you the truth," I gave her a smirk, trying to joke.

Hell, I wanted to check in on Winski.

"I don't know, Mikey..."

"Please? Let's be honest. You probably know what my kid wants more than I do. What he needs." That, and I would love to take her to lunch. Try to tear down her guard.

Get her to open up.

Molly's face contorted in thought.

"After school, he can go to the Prescott's. Hang out with Brandon."

"You just said you thought Caleb was going to be out."

"He's not going to drag is twenty kids to Winski's place. Not with Callie ten months pregnant."

Molly was smiling now, those dimples in her cheeks, and was clearly amused. "Four kids. Eight months."

God, I loved her smile. "Whichever. Please, Moll?"

Her smile fell, and her sigh was exasperated...but still, she answered, "Fine."

"Great. I'll get Anderson to school, then how about you meet me here at ten?"

"How about I meet you at the mall at ten?" Molly countered.

Not exactly what I was aiming for, but if it was going to be a make or break stipulation... "Sure. Ten. At Westfield Horton Plaza."

Molly was frowning again. "That's on the other side of town, Mikey. And I don't know the last time you've been there, but there are far better malls."

"I wanted to stop at the Gaslamp Quarter. Quicksilver and Urban Outfitters."

"Urban Outfitters is at Fashion Valley."

I could tell I wasn't winning this argument. So much for stopping for lunch in the Quarter. "Fine. Fashion Valley. Ten. Outside of Macy's."

CHAPTER SEVEN

MOLLY

I was half-tempted to show up at the mall in my CrossFit clothes.

Why did I agree to this? Why did I say, "Sure, yeah, let me cancel my plans for the day and hang out with you?"

Not that I had many plans.

Just a morning CrossFit class, then perhaps a long soak in my tub, followed by popcorn and Netflix in clean gym clothes—because life wasn't comfortable unless in leggings and a sport bra.

But nope.

No soak—instead I took a fast shower.

No sport bra—I put on a damn real bra.

With an underwire and everything.

Fucking Mikey.

I didn't bother drying my hair though.

Mikey didn't need that much time and attention.

Besides, I didn't exactly have time for it, either.

When I pulled into the parking lot outside of Macy's just a few minutes past ten, I saw Mikey's car at the back of the lot.

So of course, I parked a few rows away from his pretty white Tesla.

It was a gorgeous day for December in San Diego, I thought, crossing my arms over my chest as I walked. I probably could have grabbed a sweater to wear over my oversized long-sleeve shirt, but I got warm quickly, especially on Cross Fit days.

My knee-high boots had the slightest of heels; enough of a heel to make a faint *click* as I walked through parking and toward the mall.

There, standing to the right of the automatic sliding doors, in a brown—freaking *brown*—hoodie and dark-washed jeans, was the one I was here for.

Nope. Here for Anderson.

Why did Mikey have to be so...*pretty*?

His hair was a mess of waves on the top of his head, the brown slightly darker now that it was winter. He wore sunglasses on his face, so even though I couldn't *see* him looking at me, I could *feel* him watching me.

Knew that he'd spotted me.

I could apologize for being late...

But I wasn't going to.

"Hey, Moll," he greeted me when I was within twelve feet of him. His voice was a smooth tone that washed over me.

I was assaulted with memories.

So many damn memories.

And not one of them had to do with my late best friend.

His strong back, muscles rolling, as I watched through the door.

His hands, gripping mine and holding them to the bed as he hovered over me.

His lips at my neck.

That smooth, sexy voice in my ear...

I swallowed hard. "Mikey." I didn't stop by him; didn't want to take in the smell of his fancy cologne.

I stepped right to the automatic sliding doors and into Macy's. "Do you have an idea of what you want to get him?"

Mikey was right beside me. "I figured some clothes. New skates. Kid has this thing for bright green tape, so figured that could go in his stocking."

"What about for fun?" I slowed my walk, not really sure if we were shopping in the department store, or if he'd just wanted to meet here.

"He plays hockey for fun."

I shook my head. "No, he plays hockey because he idolizes you and his best friends play, too. He plays hockey because it gives him something to do. He watches Marvel movies for fun. He plays video games for fun."

"Okay. Then something like that, too."

I glanced over at him. Surely, he wasn't clueless over his own son...

Mikey's was looking ahead but he had the smallest of grins on his face.

Of course, he caught me looking at him. "I know that he likes the Avengers, Moll. It's the only movie series the kid watches."

That tease in his voice...

I had a feeling this was going to be a long morning.

Surprisingly enough, I had a lot of fun shopping with Mikey.

I saw a different side to him as we walked around the outdoor mall. He was lighter. Joked more. Put on floppy hats and bug-eye glasses and pretended to be a hipster in some stores. I couldn't remember a time I'd *ever* seen Mikey so lighthearted.

Not even when I'd first met him.

He was lighter then, yes. He'd always happy, yeah.

But this was a grown-up version and still...

Different.

I shouldn't like it so much.

As Mikey grabbed items from Abercrombie, and Apple, and Quiksilver, he asked for my opinion, and I helped pick out items that I knew Anderson would prefer. We even stopped at the adjacent AMC and grabbed a gift card there, for another stocking stuffer.

Which had been my idea. It was supposed to be my gift to Anderson, because going to the movies was our "thing" but any item I tried to buy, Mikey took from me and paid for himself.

"I'm getting him something!" I said, finally putting my foot down after we walked out of the freaking *Lego* store. He wouldn't even let me buy Anderson the newest kit he'd been looking at!

"We'll put your name on some of these things," Mikey answered, walking us back toward Macy's.

"You don't need to buy presents for me, Mike."

He had the audacity to grin.

Ass.

Instead of walking into Macy's though, Mikey moved to settle on one of the available benches, dropping the bags he carried to the ground.

Guy wouldn't even let me carry anything other than this small bag from Quiksilver, that held *one* shirt.

"Sit down, Moll."

Grumbling, I did.

My reaction made the man laugh.

Ass.

Hole.

"You know, Moll," he said, slouching back into the bench and stretching his long legs out in front of him. "You only call me Mike when you're pissed at me. And you're the only person in the entire world to do it."

"So?" I pulled on the front of my shirt after it got wedged between my hip and thigh from crossing one leg over the other.

"Just an observation." He crossed his arms over his chest and continued to look ahead of him, a slightly cocky grin on his face. He wasn't quiet long. "You know when you first started to get super irritated with me?"

"What is this, Mikey?" I asked, frowning at him.

I knew exactly when my like of the man turned to irritation.

Irritation at him.

Irritation at being attracted to him.

And because I was irritated, it was no longer fun I was feeling, and the tone of my words let him know that. "First you want to fire me, but before you do, you want to take a walk down memory lane? You want to rehash the last ten years? I mean, today's been surprisingly good; knew it wasn't going to last. We don't do *good*."

"Oh. We do good." Now Mikey pulled himself up and turned his upper body to face me, pushing his sunglasses up to the top of his head. "We do good really well. Let's talk about the good." He wouldn't...

"I don't know what you're talking about."

"I'm talking about when you're not avoiding me."

Now it was my turn to slouch. "I don't avoid you."

"You have been."

"Yeah, because you said you were going to fire me!"

"I didn't say that."

"No, you did. You said—"

"I said we needed to talk about your job."

"Which basically means you're going to fire me!" I fought to keep my voice low to not be overheard, even though I wanted nothing more than to yell them.

"Not exactly."

"What the hell does that mean?"

He didn't answer right away.

No, he looked at me—at my face—long and hard. So long, I had to stop from squirming in my seat. Why was he starting at me like that?

However, I couldn't just let him stare.

No.

I had to stare back.

Try to make him as uncomfortable as I was feeling.

But as I stared at him, I noticed things.

Things like the man had freckles. Not many, not as many as his son, but they were there.

Light, but there.

And things like how his green eyes were oddly darker right now.

I could remember one other time that his eyes took on that hue...

It was quick.

One moment he was staring at me across the kitchen counter, and the very next, he was pressed against me, his hands cradling my face as his mouth...

God, his mouth...

I'd only imagined how his lips would feel against mine, but the real deal was so much better than imagination.

His lips pressed against mine, then he sucked, bit, nibbled. Eventually I opened my mouth and God...his tongue was brushing over mine, and mine was in his mouth, and...and...and...

He pulled back, just enough for his eyes to search mine.

Those pretty green eyes of his were dark...

With desire.

I didn't need to feel the hard press of his cock to my stomach to recognize the want in his eyes.

I swallowed hard and realized...

My   goodness,   I   wanted   him   too.

I jerked myself back from the memory before things got embarrassing.

Before my memory brought me further into what happened next—when he had my hand in his, leading me to his room.

To his bed.

His body doing things to mine...

Mikey brushed his thumb over my lips and I jumped, startled.

And realized my lips were parted.

I pinched them together and ground my molars together.

"You still feel it."

It was all he said.

"I don't know what you're talking about," I forced out,

turning my head, looking away—far away—from him.

But I could feel him.

Then I really *could* feel him, as he took his hand and turned my head, so my face was to his once again.

"I don't want to fire you, Molly, but I do want to talk about this thing that's between us. Has been between us. And it's not something we can explore while I'm paying you."

Of course, I had to go on the defensive. "There's nothing between us."

"Where did your head just go to?"

"Mike…"

His lips quirked to the side.

"…ey," I finished.

His grin only widened.

"I'll tell you where mine went to. It went to—"

I lifted my hand and pushed my fingers to his lips. Too late, I realized my mistake.

Or maybe, subconsciously I *wanted* to feel their fullness to my fingertips.

Mikey moved his lips, just slightly, but it was enough to send nervous energy racing through my body, settling…

Settling between my thighs.

"So, you're going to let me go so you can sleep with me, and then because things will be awkward once again, I'll leave…again…but because Anderson is old enough, you won't have to beg me to come back."

I tried to move my hand before he could speak—the feel of his lips moving over my sensitive fingertips was too much—but he gently circled my wrist before I could. "It wouldn't be awkward." He lifted my hand enough to press a kiss to my palm. If I thought my fingertips were sensitive to his lips, I wasn't prepared for those lips to the center of my hand.

"But you'd still ask me to leave," I forced out, trying to keep my eyes locked on his.

"I didn't say that." He moved my wrist back and I curled my fingers down, my nails pressing hard into my palm. But then he went and kissed my wrist, and I had to stop myself from wiggling in my spot.

He had no idea what he was doing to me…

Or, maybe he did.

The glint in his eyes said he did.

"Mikey, it was a mistake." My words were whispered because…

God, I hadn't wanted it to be a mistake.

After seeing him love Trina with everything he had, after watching him crumble to the ground only to fight to be the strong father he could be for his son, after watching him stand taller than he ever had before losing Trina…

I'd wanted him.

I'd ached for him.

When I'd first met him, no, it wasn't wanting *him* but rather, wanting the same thing he gave my friend. The love. The adoration. Surely, he wasn't a one of a kind guy.

Then, when I'd been with Curtis, I'd ached for my fiancé to treat me the way I'd seen Mikey treat Trina.

But Curtis couldn't give me that.

That morning, when Mikey had taken my face in his hands and kissed me like his life depended on it…

I'd simply.

Wanted.

Him.

I wanted the rush of emotions he sent me through.

I wanted the feel of his body over and around mine—I wanted that private moment I'd spied on, but I wanted it to be more personal.

And he gave that to me.

He gave me…

Sex.

Raw.

Real.

I'd never felt more wanted than I did when I was in his arms…

Until he said Trina's name.

And I knew...

I never wanted to take my friend's place.

And Mikey would never be able to move on from the one woman he loved with his entire being.

I wasn't going to be second place.

I wasn't going to be his second choice, the one he was with only because he *literally* could not be with the one he wanted to be with.

I deserved better than that.

And the best way to move on from that day was to realize just what I'd told him—

It was a mistake.

I shouldn't have been in his bed with him.

I was never going to be more to him than a warm body to sink into, and because of that, I'd put myself firmly into employee zone.

He wouldn't cross that line.

The man was too honest for that.

If there was one thing Mikey was good at, it was keeping morals and ethics in place.

"It wasn't a mistake," Mikey said softly before bringing his face near, his lips nearly brushing my ear. To anyone passing by, it looked like he was sharing a secret with me. "Not a mistake, Moll."

"It was," I answered stubbornly, but still, didn't pull away. His face was close enough that I could feel his breath over my skin. I had to fight from falling back into memories. "You didn't want me there."

"Lies. I wanted nothing more than you there, in my bed, in that moment." He confirmed we were thinking about the same day.

The same morning.

The same moment.

"That's not how I remember it."

"Let me tell you how I remember it..."

CHAPTER EIGHT

MIKEY

I sat at the kitchen counter, nursing a cup of coffee as I waited for Molly to get back from dropping Anderson off at school and her daily Cross Fit session. I may have gotten home late last night after an away game, but I had another game tonight— we had a game damn near every Friday night—so she'd be back.

She'd come back and do house things while I went to morning skate, then she'd leave the house while I napped; come home after picking up Anderson and right before I had to leave for the arena. She'd give me enough time to hang out with Anderson, but then I'd leave for the game, and she'd feed my eight-year-old before bringing him to the game closer to game warm-ups.

It was what we did.

What we'd been doing for years.

And we were coming up on the anniversary of all of that; we were getting closer to the holidays...

Fuck, I hated the holidays.

I didn't bother looking over my shoulder to see the giant tree Molly put up for Anderson's benefit.

It was the same damn artificial tree Trina bought. Molly kept good care of it; couldn't tell that the thing was damn near eight years old, but I knew it was the tree she and my wife had picked out.

Every year, she put the tree up even though every year, no one was in the house on Christmas day to enjoy it. Anderson and I would be heading up to Quebec after the game Tuesday, for a short two-day stay. It made more sense to go up than for both the Gagnons and Perris to come down.

I wondered if Molly would want to head up, too; see the Perris again...

Curtis.

Fucking Curtis.

Still hadn't married Molly.

When I last asked her about when she'd need time off for a wedding, she shrugged it off. "Still working out the details. Enjoying being engaged, you know?"

No, I hadn't known.

Trina and I had hardly been engaged. I married her the moment I could.

Because I'd loved her that hard.

That deeply.

Damn, I missed her.

I focused on the hot liquid I sipped from my mug.

I missed Trina, yes.

But I was ready to move on. Ready to try and find again what I'd had with her; see if it was possible to love as deeply as I had once before.

And if there was one person in the world I knew Trina would approve of...

It was Molly.

But fuck me, I couldn't have her. Not with some other man's ring on her finger.

I heard the door open in the mudroom and put my coffee mug down. "Hey, Moll," I called out. I stood from my stool and moved to the other side of the counter, pulling down a second coffee mug to fill for her.

She liked it black, where I took mine with cream.

It made me grin. Molly was no wilting flower.

Dark, bold coffee, to follow her hour-long sessions at the gym.

She was a beast.

When she still hadn't left the mudroom, I called out again. "You leave?" I joked.

I heard the dryer door slam shut.

Ah. Laundry.

When she came out and passed through the living area, I noted how tired she looked. She needed the few days break that the holidays offered.

"Coffee?" I asked, putting the mug of black coffee down on the counter top and pushing it toward her as she stopped.

"Thank you," she answered softly. Up close, I could see that it wasn't tired that she looked, but sad.

"You okay?"

She shrugged and pasted a smile on her face. "Yeah. I'm golden."

"Your sarcasm is coming out," I tried joking.

Molly picked up her mug and took a cautious sip from it. It was only when she was lowering the mug that I noticed...

Molly wasn't wearing her ring.

Frowning, I tore my eyes from her hand and took in her face.

Her eyes were red-rimmed and while they weren't swollen now, there was enough evidence in her eyelids that they had been before.

"Molly?"

She must have realized what I'd noticed, because she waved her left hand in the air dismissively. "It's fine. Honest."

But that last word was almost choked off.

"What happened?"

She just shook her head, obviously not up to talking about it.

I could leave well enough alone.

I should leave well enough alone.

But damn me and my curiosity.

"Molly."

She sighed heavily and, with her eyes averted to the side, spoke softly. "We got into another fight at the gym. He wasn't thrilled with the idea of me still staying here. He's been trying to get me to quit for a few months, but I honestly thought it would blow over."

It was my turn to frown. "You gave up your engagement because of Anderson?" That wasn't necessary. He—shit, we— would have missed her, but we'd have figured it out.

She shook her head, still avoiding eye contact. "No. I gave up my engagement because my fiancé was irrationally jealous," she said, not sounding sad now, but pissed. "I gave up my engagement because my fiancé wanted me to completely change my life for him. I gave up my engagement because my fiancé wanted me to let go of—" She quickly cut herself off, dropping her chin to her chest.

"Let go of what?"

She shook her head, avoiding me. Avoiding the question.

The timing was terrible but dammit, I'd just been thinking that had she not worn a ring on her finger, I'd talk to her. See if she could ever think of me like I often thought of her.

So, while it was wrong of me—so fucking wrong of me—I saw an opportunity and decided to take it, damn the consequences.

I cleared the few feet between us and took Molly's face in my hands, bringing her face up and away from her chest, forcing her to look at me. I studied her eyes, watched as the amber depths focused, watched as her lips parted on a breath.

Watched as she realized what was coming next.

I gave her those moments.

I let her figure it out.

I let her eyes search mine, then drop to my lips…only to immediately come back to my eyes.

And then I claimed her mouth with mine.

She tasted of coffee and chocolate; her face, smooth beneath my rough hands.

I wanted more.

I needed more.

Lifting my face from hers, I took in her expression.

Everything there echoed what was going on in my own mind.

Shock. Want. Need.

Slowly, I dropped my hands to her shoulders then danced my fingers down her arms, my thumbs pressing gently into the crook of her elbow, before trailing further down until her hands were in mine. I squeezed once.

She didn't pull back.

"Molly?"

Her jaw bunched.

Her throat worked.

But her whiskey-colored eyes remained on mine. "Yes." The added nod was the clarification I needed.

With her hand in mine, I led her to my bedroom.

There wasn't a word spoken, but we were on the same page. All it took was one more look, one more gaze.

It wasn't long before she was in my arms, skin to skin, her legs wrapped around my hips as I drove into her, reveling in her slick heat. Our mouths and bodies doing the only communication needed.

Unlike every time I slept around and felt like I was cheating on my dead wife, being with Molly felt...

Right.

Only one other person had given me this same sense of completeness.

And after, after we'd both dozed off, I awoke...

Alone.

I pulled away from Molly's ear.

Just giving her my recollection, telling her in soft spoken words, had my body itching again, dying for that closeness once again.

A closeness I still hadn't been able to find in another woman's body.

"And then you were gone."

Much like the day she'd told me of her broken engagement, Molly's chin dropped to her chest. "It was a mistake," she whispered again.

"It was not a mistake." I would hold that until the day I died.

Being with Molly was *not* a mistake.

She lifted her head, her mouth opening, but whatever she had to say she thought better of, instead pinching her lips tight and shaking her head.

"There's one thing I've been curious of though, Moll."

She didn't bother loosening her lips. "Hmm?"

"What else did Curtis want you to let go of?"

Molly stared at me, her eyes flittering between mine as she decided what to say. I should have known she would avoid the question...which only had me even more curious. "We can't do this, Mikey. It wouldn't be good for Anderson."

"You're using my son as an excuse."

"Did you not use him as an excuse too?" Her brows were raised in challenge.

"No."

She nodded a few times. "You did. You said he was getting too old, so why not fire Molly so you can sleep with her again. As if she wanted to sleep with you." God, her attitude did things to me. Her sarcasm; the heat she had when she was irritated, or confused, or hurt. "You assume a lot, Michael Leeds."

She stood from the bench and, before she could storm off, I stood too, grabbing her hand. "Admit it wasn't a mistake."

"It was a mistake!"

"Admit. It wasn't. A mistake."

"Mikey, let go of me." There was no fight in her voice as she tugged on her arm.

I lowered my voice again, stepping in close and dropping my lips toward her ear once again. I liked this close proximity. I liked talking to her like what I had to say was a secret.

While the words *were* just for her, I wouldn't mind the world knowing I wanted Molly Attwood.

"It wasn't a mistake. It was five years in the making. You leaving my bed was the mistake."

"She was my best friend." Molly's voice was soft, but raw, and when I lifted my head I saw that her eyes were swimming with tears. "My very best friend. My sister, even. You are her husband."

"Was. I was her husband. She is dead, Molly."

"Yeah, from an accident you blamed me for, for years!"

"That was grief talking, and you know it." I ached to brush her unfallen tears from her cheeks.

"But you still blamed me and know what?" Her throat bobbed as she swallowed hard again, her eyes nearly overflowing with those unshed tears. Then, with a shrug of her shoulder, she blinked slowly, finally sending a tear down her cheek. "I blame me too."

CHAPTER NINE

MIKEY

When she pulled away that time, I let her. Partly because I recognized her need for space, but also because I couldn't wrap my head around the fact that Molly blamed herself.

Had she always felt that way?

Or did I place that burden on her?

The woman walked quickly though, and she was already through the doors of Macy's by the time I scooped up the day's shopping trip. My stride was longer than hers, and it wasn't long before I was within six feet of her.

Still.

I gave her space.

Not once did she look back over her shoulder, but she did keep her arms crossed over her middle as she moved through the store, toward the escalator.

As she began the downward descent, she dropped her chin again. I boarded the moving staircase just behind her, maneuvering all my bags to one hand. She stood still, not climbing down the escalator, so it was then that I closed the last of distance between us.

When I put my hand around the back of her neck, she hardly startled. She did, however, tighten her arms. I gently squeezed in support, telling her I was there before dropping my hand back to my side.

At the bottom, she didn't dart off ahead of me. I took the opportunity to walk her to her car in silence.

I wasn't sure what to do when we got to her car. She wouldn't be coming back to the house—Anderson was gone for the day and wouldn't be back until after dinner. While he was at school and then the Prescott house, I wanted to stop and see Winski, but otherwise, I was going to be home for the night. It wasn't a night for Molly to be at the house.

Nor would she be around in the morning; I'd take Anderson to school, go to morning skate, come home, nap...

She'd pick him up from school and bring him to the house, but not until before I had to leave for a home game. Molly and Anderson would come to the game and I'd maybe see my son for a few minutes after, but the team would be boarding a bus to head to the airport shortly after for our last east coast trip of the calendar year.

I'd be gone through Sunday night.

I couldn't leave this moment with Molly like this.

Not when she was clearly upset.

Sad.

Why did she blame herself? was now my first question, followed by the original, *What else had Curtis asked her to give up?*

"You don't have to walk me to my car," Molly finally spoke up. "I'm only a few rows back from you."

"Want to."

Her sigh was her only answer, but finally she loosened her arms from their tight hold.

"I'm going to visit Trevor. He's home now," I broke into the silence. "Would you want to come? You talk to Callie, right?"

Her answer was short—in length and tone. "Sometimes."

Okay...

Molly made a turn, moving between cars, and I followed closely behind.

"Did you have plans for the day?"

She shook her head, still otherwise ignoring me.

Turn around.

Leave it alone.

Count your losses.

I stopped in the middle of the lot. "Molly." My tone was exasperated but only because I was irritated with myself.

Not with her.

She turned then, and I could have sworn she rolled her eyes. Molly.

At twenty-nine years old, *rolled* her eyes at me. "What, Mikey?"

"Why are we doing this?" I asked with a shrug of my shoulders. "Why are we running around this? Things get uncomfortable, and someone pushes away. Yes. I will admit to pushing you away, but dammit, Molly, you're the best thing for Anderson. He loves you. Trina loved you. You are the person who makes my house *function*. If keeping you on as Anderson's nanny is the only way I'll keep seeing you, then I guess I'll take it. My kid's going to be twenty and in college, and I'm going to have to find a reason for you to come to the house," I tried to joke, but it was painful—both unfunny and hell, the thought of her not being around *hurt*.

"I can't do this, Mikey," Molly answered softly, shaking her head. "I can't. I won't. I'm sorry." She turned and hurried to her car, and for a moment, I considered letting her go.

Letting this end.

Here.

In a parking lot, not even three weeks from Christmas.

From the anniversary of my life going to shit.

I mean, it was only poetic that my life continued to take dives this time of year.

"I blame me too."

Hell, no.

I wasn't letting her go on that note.

Fuck the rest of the noise; I wasn't letting that one go.

Nine years was a damn long time to hold that kind of burden, and Molly didn't deserve it.

I took a long stride forward, then another, reaching Molly's car as she pulled open the door, sliding inside.

Before she could pull the door shut, I reached for it even though I was closer to the hood of her car. Releasing the bags where I stood, I moved to round her door, standing in front of her.

Molly looked up at me and, obviously resigned, put her hands her lap. "What, Mikey?"

"Why do you blame yourself?"

"Mikey…"

"Why, Moll? Why do you blame yourself?" I towered over her, my left hand with a tight grasp on her door and the other, flat-palmed to the roof. "Because of me? Because things I said? I didn't mean them. Not then. Sure as hell not now."

"I don't want—"

"Molly. It was an *accident.*"

"I should have been the one driving. I should have been with her. You've said."

"Screw what I've said, Molly. You weren't there. You couldn't have stopped her from hitting the black ice. You could not have stopped it."

Molly shook her head, turning her face to the inside of the car as she did so. "You don't understand."

I kneeled then, dropping my hands so I still held on to the door, but on the inside, and the other to my thigh. "Make me understand. There is no reason for you to blame yourself. None."

She tightened her jaw, but still refused to turn her head.

"Okay." I shrugged, not that she could see. "Then tell me what else Curtis wanted you to give up. Why did you give up your engagement? Because I'm starting to think it was Anderson. Me, even. Yeah." I nodded, pieces falling together. "Because of me? You know damn well there's some sort of energy between us. It's why you run any time it gets too real."

"I wasn't the one calling out Trina's name in my sleep," she scoffed, and I almost missed it. Almost.

"I did not."

Now, Molly turned her face back toward mine. She wore her irritation well. "You did. You murmured her name and I realized…" She shook her head. "That's why I left. Because as much as I craved the way you made me feel, I will never be Trina. And I don't want to be Trina. Trina was one of a kind. She was beautiful, and special, and damn near perfect."

"Yeah," I agreed. "She was one of a kind. But you know something, Moll? She. Chose. You." I had to force myself to keep my hands to myself instead of grabbing for her hand, holding her tight. "What does that tell you? *She chose you*. If she was one of a kind, and she was special, don't you think she only chose the best of hearts to be part of hers? Yes, Trina was special. And beautiful. But, Moll. You are too."

Molly shook her head, resorting to a quick roll of her eyes before she closed them.

"Her accident wasn't your fault."

With her eyes still closed, blocking me out, she answered, "It should have been me."

"Why? Why do you think that? Because she left behind her family; me? Because she left behind Anderson?"

At my son's name, her eyes opened again. Those whiskey-amber eyes of hers…

"Don't you wonder what he would be like if he knew her?" she asked, taking the conversation off of her. "What of hers he'd have picked up on?"

"To be honest, I think he'd be more of a shit," I said honestly, with a smile. "He'd be more like me."

"He's already just like you."

Now I did reach for her hand. "Yeah, and he's got pieces of you, too."

Molly frowned at that, and I shook her hand a little. "Don't tell me you haven't seen his sarcastic side."

"He's not sarcastic. He's stubborn. Like you."

"No. Like *you*."

"I'm not stubborn."

I leveled her with a look.

"I'm not!"

"You've avoided a question for going on ten minutes."

"It's not relevant."

"Stubborn."

She sighed again, and I saw as everything broke down inside her. Her entire demeanor changed as she slouched in the driver's seat.

"Question one. Why I blame myself," she said, her words sounding mechanical. "I didn't survive the flight from San Diego to Quebec well and had a killer headache. The Perris didn't have anything that would help—Tylenol does nothing for my headaches—so I was going to head to a pharmacy. But between the roads and not knowing where I was and the fact I was having brightness issues, Trina said she would. And she took Anderson with her because he was teething and crying and my head…"

"That's not—"

"Question two," she continued, interrupting me. Her hand tightened beneath mine, but she didn't remove it. "He wanted me to give up the only family I had left. And then you and me…we had to go and ruin—"

Family.

The only family she had left.

It made sense then, why she never went back to Minnesota. Why she stuck around San Diego throughout the year, never asking for time off to go home.

It made sense too, why the idea of losing Anderson obviously scared her so much. Why she avoided talking to me after I blurted I needed to talk to her about her job.

And it made even more sense why she kept finding herself back at my house, no matter how many times she pushed away, I pushed away…

I rose from my kneeling, leaning into her car and cutting off her words. I registered the widening of her eyes, the quick gasp from her lips, but still, within moments, claimed her mouth with mine.

CHAPTER TEN

MOLLY

Mistake, mistake, mistake…

Then Mikey changed the kiss.

Still light.

Still bordering on timid.

Unsure, even.

But with the smallest of nibbles to my bottom lip, I was gone. I opened my mouth and when his tongue brushed over mine, the same moment that I put my hand to the back of Mikey's head, there was a shift of energy.

Right, right, right…

Trina.

A whimper escaped my mouth, at the same moment that Mikey pulled back slightly, only enough to breath new air. He was on his way back in, ready to take my mouth again, when that whimper came out.

He didn't pull back.

But his eyes locked in on mine.

"I can't," I managed to whisper, as everything inside me tightened.

Tightened so tightly, it was ready to burst.

My heart, because I wanted this.

My head, because I knew it was wrong.

My tears, because I wanted… I needed… But,

I.

Couldn't.

Have.

"We can," Mikey answered, brushing his thumb over my cheek, cupping the side of my face gently.

"It's wrong, Mikey."

Mikey sighed, dropping his head forward, and I stared at the top of this head, at the waves of hair that I wanted to brush my hands through.

Finally, he looked back up, dropping his hand from my face but only so he could grab my hand.

"Anderson loves you. He needs you. Even if you're not around all the time, but he needs you. I…" He shook his head. "I honestly don't know how our house would run without you in it, but that's not your job, Moll. I want you. I've spent too long fighting it, and then pretending things hadn't shifted between us, but they did, and they only made me want you more. It's funny—" *funny enough, his voice didn't sound comical*, "I've been on dates. I've tried to move on. But the one thing my girlfriends or dates have all said, is that they feel like they're competing with a ghost. But Molly, the only one who would possibly be competing with a ghost, is you. But you're *not*. You. Are. Not." He squeezed my hand harder after the last word. "Those other women? They were competing with you. And it took our one morning together for me to realize that."

I couldn't say anything.

Had nothing to say to that.

Surely, he didn't mean it.

He'd been *so* in love with Trina.

So very much in love.

You didn't just…move on from that.

With her friend, at that.

He squeezed my hand again, gently this time, before standing. "Anderson and I will see you tomorrow."

I was frozen in my seat, not even reaching for the open door, but Mikey apparently had that covered. He shut my door softly and stepped away, back the few feet to where he'd left his bags.

Snapping back to it, I shook my head and forced myself to pull out my keys, starting my car. When I looked back up, Mikey was gone.

What are you up to?

I stared at my phone after picking it up, the ping of the incoming text breaking into my otherwise *very* quiet apartment.

After leaving Mikey at the mall, I'd run home to change, heading to a second Cross Fit class. I needed the burst of movement to clear my head. However, the session didn't last nearly long enough, and I made it back to my empty apartment.

Hours to spare before it was an acceptable time to go to bed.

I didn't want to watch television.

Didn't want to mindlessly scroll through Facebook.

Damn Mikey.

Damn him.

I looked back at the message from Asher, just as she texted me again.

I have Emersyn for the day and Porter's with Cael/JJ. I have errands and need a girl's opinion.

I laughed at that.

Well, I needed something to do…

I have time, I answered.

Asher was quick to respond. *Great! Awesome. I'm going to sneak out before the girls wake from nap. I'll pick you up in fifteen.*

Shoot. That wasn't a lot of time.

Quickly I raced through a shower and putting on real clothes—aka, clothes that didn't see a gym. I was finishing a single French braid when I saw Asher pull her big SUV into a parking spot in front of my apartment.

I locked up and went out to meet her. The moment I pulled open the passenger door, she turned down the radio—an old Ray Lamontagne song blaring through the speakers.

"Thank you for agreeing to come with," Asher said as I settled in the leather seat. "I don't have a clue..." She shook her head, laughing at herself.

"What don't you have a clue about?"

"This stupid dress-up event the team is putting on. Didn't you hear?"

I shook my head, turning in my seat so I could talk with her. "No. What 'stupid dress-up event'?"

With both of her hands on the wheel, Asher maneuvered the SUV out of my apartment complex and toward the main freeway.

"I mean, I shouldn't call it stupid. It's a really great thing and if Porter heard me say it was stupid, he'd probably—"

"Asher."

She stopped and took a breath.

"So, you know the team does the charity hockey game at the beginning of the season for Bri."

I nod but let her continue.

"With everything happening with Ryleigh—" Asher had to pause, and I saw her scrunch her face in all directions, no doubt fighting the tears that were evident in her eyes. "The boys decided to do something big. Bigger than Casino Nights, and Dining with the Team nights. Both do incredibly well, but they wanted to do something for mom."

Now I was fighting my own tears. I didn't really know Ryleigh Prescott—other than maybe a handful of times she'd been up in the box during games, over the years. But I did know her sons well.

"That's really sweet."

Asher nodded, swallowing hard. When she spoke again, her voice was clear. "So I need a new dress. I have a black one for Casino Night, and another black one for dining and awards and whatever else I'm supposed to show up at, but this is going to be like a gala. I mean, they're calling it a Gala. I was going to ask Sydney for her opinion but she's pregnant and busy and all of that. And we both know I'm a bit of a loser and don't actually talk to the other wives." She laughed lightly, and I rolled my eyes jovially at her.

"You're so full of it Asher. Everyone likes you; you're just hard to open up."

"I prefer a small circle of friends," she justified.

"Me too." Even though I wasn't in the spotlight—at all—compared to Asher and her family, I knew that the life of a hockey player's family was often on display. The Enforcers were very homey compared to other teams; we didn't have any players who were dating A-list actresses. TMZ wasn't horribly interested in the guys, either. But I could remember how interested everyone was in Asher and Porter when they first started dating.

I understood her need to keep her circle small.

And while I got along with everyone, I was happy to be included in Asher's circle.

"So, what did Porter have to say about you needing a new dress? Surely the man wouldn't have *made* you get a new one."

"He doesn't know," she answered sheepishly.

"Then why is this such a big deal?" I asked with a loud laugh and bigger smile.

She shrugged with just one shoulder, a small smile on her face, without answering for a few beats. Finally, "You know he and I didn't do the big wedding. He helped me pick the other two dresses—which, I'll have you know, are the only fancy things in my closet. I kinda wanted to surprise him, like girls do for their husbands at the wedding. It's been a hard few months for him so…"

Smiling, I tipped my head back to the headrest. "Asher, I love you."

Her laugh, husky and light, filled the SUV. "Love you too, friend."

Being on the outside, I watched a lot of relationships through the years. I was envious of them all. Most loved like Mikey had loved Trina.

Porter and Asher's relationship was different.

Theirs was the most fun to watch—mostly because they were seemingly so different. He was loud and a jokester, running his mouth whenever the time called for it. She was reserved, a thinker. Sometimes Porter would say or do something that would piss her off, and she wasn't afraid to give him the silent treatment.

But they were always back to good the next time I'd see them.

Because they loved just as hard as Trina and Mikey, Caleb and Sydney, Trevor and Callie...

"You should come," Asher said a few minutes later, after driving in silence. "I can get you a ticket."

"I'm sure that the tickets cost a fortune. Hence, the reason for doing the whole thing."

"No, no. Not like a guest. But as part of the team. Keep me company when Porter is mingling."

I smiled over at her, sure she was joking. "You can mingle, too. Besides, when we're done with you today, Porter's not going to want to take you off his arm."

"Promises, promises," Asher teasingly chided. "Be my friend and come."

"I am your friend."

"Which means you'll come."

"I didn't—"

"I think you'd look good in red. Let's find you a red dress..."

"Asher... What about Anderson? I'm sure that Mikey will be going, and that means I'll be the one watching him."

"Sydney won't be coming. She's been having those hip and nerve issues, so she'll be home with the kids. All of them, bless her heart. I'm sticking Emersyn with her, even though Sydney said she'd be fine. And Emersyn is great with the little boys, too, so it'll be great. Anderson can hang with Brandon."

"I've pawned Anderson off on Sydney too often the last few months."

"Yeah, for like...thirty minutes a day. Besides, Brandon and Anderson are always holed up in the game room. They won't be a problem for Sydney."

"I don't know..."

"It's decided," Asher said with a wide smile, taking her eyes off the road for the smallest of moments. Her hands tightened on the wheel when she did, only to relax when facing forward again.

"And we're going to find you a red dress. It will make those natural highlights in your hair come out. I'm jealous of that, by the way."

"My hair?"

She nodded. "Yeah. It's so flowy and light..."

"Yours is thick and wavy, so, pretty sure you win."

Asher shook her head. "It's a pain. Thank God we're not in Carolina anymore. Do you know how humid it gets there? And with this monstrosity? Shoot, no wonder Porter tried dumping me..."

"One, I'm pretty sure that's *not* how the story went..."

Asher looked over the console at me again and winked with a grin.

This was the side of her that the team wives didn't see.

So, yeah.

I was happy to be in her circle.

...and I could probably be convinced to put on a pretty red dress and go to a Gala I didn't really belong at.

CHAPTER ELEVEN

MIKEY

After visiting with Callie and Trevor, the Prescotts and I headed to O'Gallaghers to decompress. Even though I didn't frequent the pub too often anymore, I needed the distraction—from the game, from the upcoming gloom and doom that my life was in December…

From Molly.

I wasn't going to push it.

Oh, who the hell was I kidding? I was going to push it.

I'd push until she either bent, or she walked away for good. And if she chose to walk away for good, I'd learn to be okay with it.

And Anderson?

He'd be okay eventually, too.

As we walked into the pub, I didn't recognize the bartender working but the boys seemed to. Called him Jake.

"Con's in the back," Jake told Caleb as we all sat at the mostly vacant bar. It was early enough in the day yet, but it wouldn't be long before people started piling in to San Diego's most popular Irish-American pub. "Want me to grab him?" The guy effortless popped caps off bottles and placed the glass down on napkins in front of us.

"Only if he's free," Caleb said, pulling his napkin toward him. O'Gallaghers was helping sponsor the Gala next week, but we didn't come here to talk business.

We came because the boys needed a break from life.

And hell, I could understand that. I could understand the loss they were preparing for. This potential loss of Trevor was only a piece of the storm that was going on in the Prescott family.

I turned in my stool so I was facing more inward toward the Prescott brothers. Jonny was next to me, with Porter on his side, and Caleb at the other end. I reached for my bottle, but only lifted it by the neck, swirling it around in circles.

Winski wasn't doing so hot.

He played it off during our visit, but before we left his wife told us about the massive migraines he'd been experiencing since being taken off the ice; the nightmares that had kept him awake overnight; the irrational bout of anger he had earlier in the day before being sent home from the hospital. When you played hockey—hell, any contact sport—you knew the risks. You knew concussions could be little things, but they could also be devastating to an athlete.

I didn't think Winski would be sitting on our bench again. The puck had been going fast, but…

Shit, with his symptoms as they were, Winski probably had some dormant concussion issues that were just being brought to light now.

"He's not coming back," Porter, always the one to say what he was thinking, blurted out, as he stared at the bar in front of him, fingers playing with the corners of the black napkin. "Shit, life fucking sucks right now," he added, quieter than his first sentence, looking up to the open industrial-type ceiling.

"The team will get through it," Cael said, nodding a few times. "Trevor's a big piece, yeah, but you're a strong team. We'll get through it."

Jonny crossed his arms over his chest, pushing his stool back slightly to rest on the back legs. "And everything else? Fuck, Cael, I'm playing like shit—"

"You're playing fine."

"And I feel like everything is going to blow up, sooner than later. Losing Winski this close to break… Hell, teams who were on the top the first half of the season, end up on the bottom the second half, with losses like this one."

I offered my insight, speaking the bit I knew was on their minds, "And with a coach, a goaltender, and a power forward who are likely to lose their mom… We're fucking screwed."

"Which is why family shouldn't be so fucking close in sports," Porter murmured, finally picking up his beer and taking a long drag.

"Whatever, Ports." Caleb started in on his youngest brother. "I'm really sick of that argument. You could have left. Your contract—"

"Enough, you two. God," Jonny cut in, shaking his head. "You two fight about fucking everything."

Caleb turned his attention to Jonny. "Don't tell me you've never gotten tired of Porter and his woe-is-me, I got traded to my family's team, speech."

"Sure, but that's Porter." Jonny was always the levelheaded one. "Has been Porter for-fucking-ever. Stop beating a dead horse."

"Timing sucks, yes," I offered, shutting down the brothers' fight. "No, it's not great that three important pieces of our team are dealing with personal things too, but guys, you built the Enforcers organization. Or, your dad started the build. You guys have made it what it is, and the city is rooting for you. You've made the organization a family one and with it, San Diego calls Prescott its family. Yeah, the next few weeks are going to suck. But it's also why we're doing this fancy-assed party next week. For Bri," I said pointedly, directly to Caleb. "And for your mom. And the city's going to show up, just like you three will; like the team will. Like the city and team have, again and again, over the years."

Just then, Conor O'Gallagher came pushing through the swinging doors, taking my attention off my grieving friends.

"Hello, boys," the tall brute said as he reached us, holding his hand out. He slapped/shook Caleb's hand—then pounded his back when Caleb stood up from his seat, as they were the closest friends—before shaking mine, Porter, and Jonny's hands.

"Mia and me will be at your shindig next Wednesday." While O'Gallaghers was sponsoring and supplying adult beverages, there would be fancy suits doing the serving. "You sure you don't want more than beer and wine? I can bring harder liquor. Even if it's just in the back for you boys. Oh," he turned his attention to me. "Speaking of boys. Meant to send you a text, but it's been chaotic at the house. Your boy is good people. My daughter can't stop talking about his heroic efforts. But," he pointed at me, his face serious even if there was a small tilt to his lips, "she's still my little girl. Your boy better keep his hands to himself."

"Your daughter's like…seven."

"Eight. Going on fucking seventeen. She's a diva, that one. Ava was a cakewalk at that age." His comments were enough to lighten the mood again, and Caleb shook his head.

"Must be the age. Brody is showing signs to be like this one," he said, pushing at Porter's shoulder. "Ports isn't even at the house that much, and Brody is emulating his uncle."

"I'm an awesome role model, thank you very much," Porter rebounded, putting a hand to his chest.

Just like that, the moment was back to good. Beer and good times, with good friends. Fixed everything.

For now.

It had been an okay-ish road trip.

Jonny didn't play Saturday or Sunday because, yeah, he was playing like shit.

We lost both Friday and Saturday's games, but pushed through Sunday just fine.

When I got back to the house Sunday night, the last thing I wanted was to see Molly packed up and ready to go, but I was prepared for the possibility.

Hell, the entire drive back from the arena to the house, I'd been expecting her to text me with an update and an *Anderson's sleeping over at the Prescott house* text.

But it was a school night.

She wouldn't send him off.

So, even though I was prepared for her to be ready to leave but hopeful she'd stick around, I was surprised when I came into the house and saw Molly in the kitchen, her back to me. She was in her sleep attire—her oversized sweatshirt that fell off a shoulder, and cotton shorts that showed off her toned thighs.

Her sleepwear told me she wasn't planning on leaving tonight.

"Hey," I said, moving to the counter. She turned and pushed a mug at me.

"Decaf."

I lifted my brows as I sat at a stool, not saying anything.

She moved, propping her back to the far counter, her hands braced beside her with her fingers curling around the edge of quartz.

And for the first time in months—hell, probably years—she stared at me.

Didn't lower her eyes.

Didn't look away.

She stared at me and I could feel that shit in my soul.

"You guys played terribly," she finally said.

I nodded, my hands cradling the mug after sipping off the top. "We did. It's going to take some adjusting."

"What's your schedule like this week? Do you need me to pick up Anderson any extra days? Will you guys have longer practices or anything?"

I shook my head. "Nah. No changes. Regular schedule applies."

She took a deep breath and I watched as her chest rose and fell with the action. "I have plans Wednesday night." Her grasp of the counter tightened. "Sydney said she was okay with Anderson staying at the house during the gala. I'm sorry."

My unexpected thrill of her being here, fell away quickly.

Of course, she was making changes to the time she had with Anderson. It was what she'd been doing lately.

"That's cool," I said instead. She had a life. And she made it clear that she thought the two of us was a 'mistake'—didn't matter what I said otherwise. She had strong feelings against it, and I couldn't change that.

It also likely meant, even though we'd had an almost heart-to-heart only a handful of days before, she was still leaving us.

Leaving Anderson, I corrected.

No.

Leaving *us*.

And the thought crushed me.

I'd loved someone enough to recognize these feelings I had for Molly.

I hadn't wanted them. No, not at first. But now, with the realization that she was leaving us, I knew that when she did, she was going to take a big part of me with her.

My heart.

And I didn't think I had it in me to find someone else after she left.

Finding love and losing it once, was hell enough.

The second time? Shit.

I wouldn't try a third time.

My heart would leave with Molly, and that would be it.

"When does your school schedule start?" I asked, taking the high road. I wasn't going to beg her to stay. Beg her to consider that maybe she could love me too.

Molly frowned. "Huh?"

"When does school start? When do I have until, to prepare Anderson for the change?"

She was still frowning.

"You're still quitting, right?"

Her frown deepened but then she shook her head, brows raised. "Sure. Yeah. Right. School. Classes start January twenty-something. I hadn't really... I'll get back to you on that."

"Yeah. Do that." I stood from the counter. "Have a good night, Moll. I can take Anderson to school so...you're welcome to stay but you don't have to."

"Yeah." Her frown was back, but I didn't have it in me to sit there and analyze it. I moved away from the counter and toward my room, but before I pushed through my bedroom door, Molly's voice stopped me.

"Mikey."

I looked back over my shoulder. She was standing near the stool I'd just vacated.

Her face a mask of confusion, she started at me—again. But then shook her head and looked down. "Never mind."

With that, I pushed into my room and closed her out.

CHAPTER TWELVE

MOLLY

"This is a terrible idea," I told my reflection, even though the words were for Asher. My head moved as the stylist did a full blow-out to my hair, but even with my eyes locked to the mirror, I wasn't seeing the stylist. I wasn't seeing me.

Heck, I was hardly even hearing the noises of the salon Asher dragged me to.

Asher, sitting beside me and getting her waves tamed into nicer curls, laughed. She was planning on a low-side pony—and had been adamant that the tail be over her right shoulder, even though her hair dresser tried talking her into the other side—something about symmetry and Asher's tattoos and ear piercings. "It's a fantastic idea. That dress… I mean, Moll, Mikey won't be able to take his eyes off of you."

I didn't hear her though. "God, if Mikey sees me, he's going to be so pissed. Pissed that I lied. Pissed that I chose some fancy venue instead of Anderson." My eyes darted over the mirror, to Asher's reflection. "He's already convinced I'm quitting to go to school—"

"Well, aren't you? You did say that if he fired you, you'd consider school."

"And this will only tell him that I don't really care about Anderson and—"

"Molly." Asher's smile was wide and her eyes, amused. "Take a breath."

"Can I return the dress? I have to return the dress. I can fix this." I'd leave here, pick up Anderson. He and I could have a pizza and Marvel night. I'd even offer to bring Brandon with! Then the boys wouldn't have to break their plans, because I was sure they were excited, and—

"You're not returning the dress. You're going to get all fancy and made up. You're going to the Gala. You're going to have a damn good time. And you're going to win over Mikey Leeds."

"He's going to be so mad..."

"Molly! Listen to me," she laughed. Asher laughed. She freaking laughed at me! "The *only* thing Mikey is going to be thinking about is how to keep you around. Promise."

I shook my head, forgetting the woman pulling my hair in every which direction.

"No. This will be the final wedge. He's going to tell me to not bother coming back after Christmas. Oh my God! That means I'll only hang out with Anderson for like...seven more days! I can't do this. I have to go." I put my hands on the chair armrests and Asher pointed to my hairdresser.

"Do not let her stand up, Stephanie." Then, Asher leaned over and slapped at my arm, barely grazing me with her fingers. "Snap together, Molly. Mikey *wants* you."

I scoffed at that.

"He does. Trust me."

"Well, yeah. I guess. I mean, yes. I know. He told me as much. But he doesn't want me forever and I'm a forever kind of gal. I can't do a fling, and I can't do a fling with my best friend's husband."

My hair dresser—Stephanie, I guess—stopped pulling at my hair and I saw her look down at me with a confused look.

"She's dead," I told her, probably a little colder than I meant, but who was she to judge me?

"I think you're selling yourself short, and that you're not giving Mikey enough credit."

"A pretty red dress isn't going to make him magically want

forever."

"Well, then… Just come out and have a good time. Hang out with me. Because I really hate these big events. And, because you already got your nails done; you can't exactly go to the gym looking all dolled up. Let's not waste the manicure, Moll."

My gut was telling me something tonight was not going to go according to plan.

I was nervous as hell. What would he think? What would he do? But…

It was one night.

"Fine."

My nervousness only grew more when Asher insisted I ride with her and Porter; and, because my car was piece of shit compared to the others that were going to be in the parking lot, I agreed.

But now I was stuck.

I fiddled with my champagne glass as I stood next to Asher at a tall, but small in diameter, round table, taking in the venue.

Excuse me.

The art museum.

The museum itself was beautiful, but the hall we were in was done up to the nines. Chandeliers. Ice sculptures.

And *white.*

White centerpieces.

White tablecloths.

White bulbs decorating the Christmas trees, strategically placed around the hall.

This was no dark affair.

Oh no.

The lights were on, the walls were white, the décor white, too. So much white.

If Mikey were to look around, he'd find me easily.

Hell, I found him the moment he walked through the doors, looking handsome as ever in his dark suit. Head to toe, black, but with a silver bow tie.

"I didn't think it would be so bright in here," I told Asher in hushed tones. There was a string quartet playing in the corner, with the occasional piano melody, but it was still relatively quiet in the room.

No one was speaking too loudly.

You could have a conversation without raising your voice.

And therefore, it was too quiet for me.

Nervously, I pulled up at the strapless top of my dress with one hand, then switched the champagne flute to my other so I could do the same on the left side.

"I didn't really either," she answered. "But I suppose. It's a *gala*. I think those are synonymous with bright and fancy."

"There's a lot of people here." I looked around. "The hall is probably at max capacity."

"Which is awesome." Asher nodded, then startled when Porter walked up behind her, sliding his hands from her hips to rest over her stomach.

He pressed a kiss in front of her ear before speaking. "You ladies having fun?"

I got to witness Porter's surprise at Asher's dress. She hadn't veered too far off from her usual dark choice, choosing a beautiful, rich green dress that made her eyes pop. The dress, like mine, was strapless, as well as floor length, but hers had an intricately beaded corset.

I'd been envious of Mikey's love for Trina.

I was wishful for the love I saw so often, in this room of hockey players and their other halves.

But what I witnessed when Porter saw Asher nearly two hours earlier?

It wasn't what I'd been expecting.

I mean, I knew the man loved his wife with everything in him. His reaction though…

It almost put to shame the adoration I'd, once upon a time, witnessed in Mikey's eyes for Trina.

And since arriving, he didn't leave Asher alone for longer than ten minutes at a time. I also realized why Asher had her pony over her right shoulder; it was because Porter favored her left side.

It was cute.

Disgustingly cute.

"The turnout is amazing," I said, looking around the room again.

Porter nodded. "It is. Mom would love it."

I wanted to ask how she was doing, but I knew this wasn't the right place for that. Earlier, Asher shared that they moved Ryleigh to hospice; it wouldn't be much longer.

Which only made the strength the Prescott family had even more profound to me.

That they could all be here—the sisters, too; I saw Avery making her way around the room a little bit before—even though their mom and dad were back in their home state of Wisconsin.

I watched my friend get a tight hug from her husband, and another kiss to the cheek, before he went off to mingle again. Asher watched him walk away, a small smile on her face but still, a touch of sadness in her eyes.

"Anyway," Asher finally said, bringing her attention back and away from Porter. "I think it's time for you to pull up your big girl thong and go find Mikey."

Her words shocked me, and I stuttered. "Excuse me?"

"Go find Mikey," she said, a push to my shoulder. "I mean, you probably know where he is. I've seen you searching the place."

"I—No, I haven't. I don't know what you're talking about." I drained the last of my champagne.

"Then let me help you out. He's staring at you."

My eyes widened at her. "He is not." But I followed her line of sight and...

There he was.

I could *feel* his stare.

It wasn't a hateful stare.

It wasn't a curious stare.

It was a...

Asher leaned in toward me and whispered, a sing-song tone to her voice. "He thinks you're gorgeous. He wants to kiss you—"

My face was bright red. "Okay, Miss Congeniality. That's enough."

"He wants to smooch you."

I backhanded-slapped at her, as Mikey began to make his way through the crowd. "Shush, Asher."

"He wants to hug you."

I may have been bright red, but Asher still got me to laugh. "Do you have that entire quote memorized? Geez, Asher."

She shrugged, a smug smile on her face. "I like me a good Sandra Bullock movie. What can I say."

"At least you weren't rain dancing to sweat dripping down…" I stopped myself, because Mikey was within hearing distance. "You know."

"Down my balls," Asher gladly finished—and Mikey had to have heard, because there was the smallest of stumbles to his steps.

"Oh my God," I mumbled, dropping my head.

Asher, laughing, rubbed her hand over my shoulder blade. "You got this. I'm going to seek out my sexy husband again. Maybe sneak up on *him* for once."

Then she was gone, and Mikey was there, and my heart tripped in my chest.

"Balls?"

Not what I was expecting to be the first words from his mouth.

"Quoting Sandra Bullock," I managed to say without croaking.

He nodded twice, slowly, before dropping his eyes down over me—even slower than his nod had been. "So. Plans Wednesday, huh?"

"Asher made me." I had my hands wound together in front of me, and I was playing with one of my gel-polished nails.

"You look beautiful."

"You do too." I shook my head. "I mean, thank you."

"Can I grab you another drink?"

I shook my head. I'd only had one, and already my mind was

swimming. I didn't need another to further cloud my thoughts.

"I'm sorry. I know I should be with Anderson—"

"No, I'm glad you're here." He rested an elbow on the table. "Really glad."

"Oh?"

He nodded, looking down at his hands—an odd showing of hesitancy. Mikey Leeds wasn't a hesitant man. "I was a bit of an ass the other night."

My brows drew together, and I shook my head.

He nodded. "I was. I keep thinking, keep *hoping*, that I can convince you that we can move forward, that this is how everything is supposed to play out, but I know you were incredibly close to Trina. I hear you when you say you don't want to disservice her memory that way. I get it. I do. But I keep having these hopes, and then I came home and you weren't ready to bolt, and I'd thought..." His voice drowned out as he looked away.

But then he was looking at me again. "I thought maybe you decided differently. But then, when you said you had plans for tonight and making plans for Anderson so you didn't have to be with him, I just immediately assumed you were still leaving."

"I was only ever planning on leaving because *you* said—"

"I know. I know." He reached for my hand, and I was too shocked to not let him take it. "I wasn't the most eloquent in my asking, no. And I will absolutely respect your decision, but I wanted to tell you..."

I held my breath, even though my lips had parted. He'd dropped his eyes again and I could feel as he played his thumb over the bumps of my knuckles.

I couldn't tear my eyes off his face though.

"I wanted to tell you that you're our family too." My gasp was barely audible, but when he looked up, his green eyes were surprisingly glassy. "It would be selfish of me to take from you what you don't want to give. And I'd hate like hell if I did something to drive you away. I would never forgive myself if I was the cause Anderson lost the only female role model he truly has. You're good for him. You're good for *us*. I know Anderson doesn't need a nanny much longer, but I still want you around. I want you to go to school, finish your degree or start one or whatever the hell you're planning, but I want to you to still be around."

"I don't..." I didn't have anything to finish that thought with.

My brain was mush.

My heart, an oversized organ in my chest, racing in an erratic pattern.

And my lungs, unable to take a full breath.

I could have sworn I heard the smallest of laughs—one I recognized and fought the need to look around the room for, even though it had a French tilt...but it couldn't be. My mind was playing tricks on me. Sending me Trina's voice at a time I was daring to think about Mikey in terms other than as my employer.

But Mikey was talking again, and I was breathing for his words.

"The house would be empty without you. Hell, it's empty whenever you're not there *now*. I want you there, Moll. Every day. The thought of you being gone..." He shook his head, frowning. I wanted to run my thumb over the ridges in his forehead, but I couldn't move. Could hardly breathe. "I want you to try. Again, that's selfish of me, but could you? Do you think you could try?"

CHAPTER THIRTEEN

MIKEY

I'd never been more nervous in my life.

Not when I left home at seventeen.

Not for my first date with Trina.

I hadn't even nervous when I proposed to her.

Moving forward in life with Trina had been easy, too easy.

Nothing—not a damn thing—was easy when it came to Molly.

But I had to lay it out. I couldn't keep pussy-footing around it.

I either admitted to us both that I wanted her, I wanted us, I wanted *tomorrow*...

The very things that I'd convinced myself I didn't want anymore, after losing Trina—I wanted with Molly.

"And if I do try? If *we* try? What happens when it ends?" Molly finally said softly.

I squeezed her hand. "You can't write it off before it's even begun."

"Mikey, you loved Trina. So much. I'm not sure you have that in you for someone else." Her voice was even softer now, and I could see in her eyes that what she said, she thought was true.

"Every time I've pushed you away," I answered back, shaking

her hand gently with each point. "Every time you've left...you've come back. That has to mean something."

"Yeah, that I've a glutton for punishment."

"Or that with me is where you're supposed to be."

"Mikey, it's not right." She shook her head and looked away.

"Why do you fight it so hard, Moll?" I asked, my voice barely over a whisper.

When she looked at me again, it was with determination on her features. "Because I refuse to lose what little I already have. Can't that be okay? Can't that be enough?"

"What are you afraid of?" I dared her.

"You said you'd let me say no."

"I need a better reason than you're scared."

"Fine," she said, purpose in her voice but tears in her eyes. God, I was suddenly tired of making her cry. "Because you won't ever love me like you loved her. And I don't expect you to."

"No, Moll, I wouldn't love you like I loved Trina," I confessed, "but I'd love you for *you*. I *love* you for you. I love you, Molly." The words were out of my mouth before I could think them, but they were true.

So damn true.

I loved Molly and had for years.

She shook her head, but her eyes filled faster, tears falling over her lower eyelids before she could even blink. I reached out to cup her face in my hands, my thumbs catching the salty drops.

"I do," I whispered roughly. "I have. God, Moll." I shook my head lightly but refused to let my eyes leave hers. "When you came to the house, what, three years ago? When you told me you were engaged? It was the second worse day of my life." She was shaking her head in my hands again. "It was. I'd finally come to realize that the reason I wasn't moving on in life was because of you, and I was convinced that the only person who would help me find love again, would be you. And that of any person in the world, any woman I would ever cross paths with, you were the one that Trina would approve of. You've been more than Anderson's nanny for years. *Years*, Molly. Do you hear me?"

Her eyes were still overfilling, tears still falling down her cheeks and catching on my thumbs, but she nodded. "Years," I said again, needing her to understand. "Anderson needs you, but dammit, Molly, I need you too."

"Because the house doesn't function without me," she tried to bite out, but her emotions didn't allow the sarcasm to hit as hard as I was sure she intended.

"An excuse, Moll." I dropped my forehead to hers, and she closed her eyes. "Life doesn't function without you. You're the voice of reason in the house. You're the reason Anderson is a damn good kid, and you know it. Yeah, we'd be able to survive without you, but I don't want to."

When she opened her eyes to look up at me, I shook my head, rocking my forehead over hers. "I don't want to."

I felt her hands timidly grab the front of my dress shirt, pulling it away, just slightly, from my body.

"Molly." I needed her to say something.

Anything.

Say something, push me away, pull me close…

Something.

When she didn't, when I lifted my head back from hers with a deep breath, she let go of my shirt.

I dropped my hands to her shoulders, taking in her tear-stained face.

I didn't want this to be the end.

I would remember her face, right here, for the rest of my life, and it would haunt me.

But then she slipped her hands over my sides, under my suit jacket, and lifted herself up.

I felt her breath before she gently brushed her soft lips to mine.

Like her hands before, her kiss was timid.

She was scared.

Hell, so was I.

I couldn't lose Molly, like I'd lost Trina.

I would not survive it a second time.

But life was about experience. You couldn't let one terrible thing hold you back. Not when you had an entire life ahead of you.

Again, I cradled her face, keeping the angle gentle as our lips played over one another softly. When Molly moved to make the kiss deeper, I groaned against her mouth, slipping a hand to the back of her head, into her gorgeous hair.

Holding her in place.

But she was holding me in place too—holding me close—with her fingers digging into my lower back. I could feel her heart beating hard against my chest, the rush and drive just as frantic as my own.

The longer she kissed me, her tongue rubbing over and around mine, the more my dick stirred to life. Not needing to sport major wood here in a room full of San Diego's finest people, I reluctantly pulled my mouth from hers, but didn't pull away far.

Instead, I pressed a kiss to her cheek, then in front of her ear, before whispering, "Come home with me tonight, Molly."

Her hands flattened against my back, and her body shivered against mine, at my words.

"Please," I added, my whispered words soft and directly to her ear. Her body shivered again, the action no match for my stirring cock.

So much for not being hard.

My cock was like granite against her stomach, and the more Molly wiggled against me in her pretty red dress...

Shit, I wanted to peel it from her slowly, exposing her body inch by inch.

The thought wasn't doing anything for my present situation.

But it was her whispered, "Okay," that really had the blood flowing south.

Thank God, Molly drove in with Porter and Asher. Not that I thought Molly would bail. Other than the few times I had to walk around the room, and I left her with Asher...Molly hadn't left my side.

I was glad to have to drive her home; I didn't want to let her out of my sight. Now that I admitted my feelings for her out loud, I wanted to keep her close.

I pulled the car into the garage, and even though I shut it off, we both stayed sitting. Neither of us unbuckling or moving to get out.

"And Anderson's at Brandon's?" Molly finally asked, glancing over at me. Her face was flushed, her eyes wide, and her hands were folded in her lap.

I nodded. "He is. I'll be picking him up in the morning. It's… You and me."

Molly began to nod, and I reached over, placing my hand over her folded ones. "We don't have to. We can just hang out."

I didn't want to just hang out.

I craved Molly.

I could remember the feel of her body underneath mine; her breasts pressed to my chest; her toned thighs gripping my sides.

I wanted it again.

And again.

I didn't want to sleep tonight. I wanted to take her in the living room, the kitchen, the bedroom, and then the shower. I wanted to look around my house and see her…see us.

I wanted her to know, come morning, that I meant what I said.

I didn't want her to doubt a single moment.

A single word.

I didn't want her to think that what I felt for her was any less than what I felt for Trina. It was different but consuming. Almost more than what I'd ever felt for Trina.

Fuck, I was so unworthy of Molly, and I would spend the rest of my life proving to her that I loved her.

Would love her.

Forever.

If she let me.

Her face screwed in question, she faced me. "It's not awkward?" She removed one of her hands from under my palm but spread her fingers of her other. When I threaded my fingers between hers, she folded hers around mine.

"Not for me." I squeezed her fingers. "Are you okay? You're sure?"

She stared at me, just as the interior light of the car dimmed to black. It wouldn't be long before even the garage light turned dark.

"I'm sure," she whispered, her eyes locked on mine.

I lifted her hand toward me, kissing the inside of her wrist, before letting her go to unbuckle. I got out of the car, leaving my suit jacket in the back, and moved around to her door in time to open it for her, and after she was out, she waited for me before heading into the house.

I followed behind her closely, hitting the garage door button as she stepped inside then, with my fingertips to her lower back, I followed her into the living room. I hit the dimmer switch on the lights and quickly pulled the lights low.

I wanted to see her.

But I liked the dimness.

Bright enough that I could see her, but dark enough to not take away any of the feelings of need, urgency, desire.

Her dress wasn't particularly exposing. Nothing incredibly fancy.

It was strapless and had the slightest of dips at her back. A dip that wasn't always on display when her hair—which was still fairly long, hanging just below her shoulder blades—cascaded down her back. But now that she'd pulled the locks over her shoulder, her left shoulder and back were on display.

Molly had been going to Cross Fit since we first arrived in San Diego, but I never really took the time to appreciate what it did to her body. She wasn't overly muscular but toned in all the right places. The slight ridges in her back, the toned cup of her shoulder, all had me itching to press kisses from her pretty brunette head, down to her toes.

Instead, I stepped closer and trailed my fingers up over the material of her dress before flattening my hand against the bare skin of her upper back. She drew a shoulder up and in at the contact but relaxed again quickly.

At the couch, I stopped her, turning her toward me. She immediately tipped her face up and when I stepped close, bringing my body flush with hers, she didn't back away. Her earlier worried expression didn't pass over her features.

No.

Molly smiled.

Timidly, but it was still a smile, and I couldn't help but give her an answering one in return. "I love you," I told her again, my voice rough with need. "But that doesn't mean we do anything you don't want to do. I don't know how..." I slid my hands down her back, my hands cupping her ass. "Shit, Moll, it's been a while."

"Just kiss me."

That I could do.

I lowered my head and she met me in the middle.

This kiss held promise.

This kiss wasn't slow. It wasn't one testing the waters.

This one clearly said where we were headed, and I was quickly hard behind my slacks once again. Molly's hands were fisted in my shirt and she was tugging it up and out of the confines of my waistband, while I moved us closer to the couch. I sat, pulling her to my lap as I lifted the skirt of her dress, and Molly arranged her legs to straddle me.

Our mouths never leaving the other's.

Teeth clashing.

Tongues brushing.

The taste of champagne on her tongue, and likely the single beer I'd had, on mine.

But it wasn't the alcohol that was intoxicating—it was Molly.

All Molly.

Her fingers worked on the buttons of my shirt and I dug my fingers into her hips, our bodies meeting in the one place I needed the most pressure. Soon she had my shirt completely undone and when her hands made contact with skin, I groaned against her mouth.

She grazed her nails down my chest as she ground her hips over my lap.

I needed…

Her skin.

I tugged on the skirt of her dress—up, up, up—until I could feel the smooth skin of her legs. I rested my hands there, curving around the sides of her thighs, but when she rolled over me again, her body moving with our kiss, I couldn't stop myself from dragging my hands further up her legs.

…Until they met bare ass.

"Fuck, Molly," I said against her mouth, and her lips curled against mine. "Off. I want this off," I issued, but kept my hands on her. I wanted her dress off but didn't want to lose contact with her.

Shit.

I needed more of her skin.

"How do we get it off you?" I squeezed her ass one last time before reluctantly letting go. The middle of the dress was too tight to go over her head. There wasn't any elastic for her to pull it down.

Which meant there was a zipper somewhere.

Where?

Molly leaned away from me, and my hands went to her back, sliding slowly to her sides, trying to find the ridge of a zipper.

"Left side," she finally directed and there it was. I found the tiny-assed zipper—shit, it was really fucking tiny—and pulled it down.

The material of her dress fell away, pooling at her hips and revealing…

Her breasts.

No bra.

"God, Molly," I managed, giving her zero time to prepare for my mouth. I leaned in and licked first one tight nipple, and then sucked the other into my mouth.

"Mikey." Her answering moan was breathless, and she was holding my head to her. I suckled on her nipple, then let it pop from my lips, only for me to immediately kiss her mouth once again.

Her breasts flattened to my chest, skin to skin. I could feel the wetness I left behind, and when Molly rolled over my again, this time dragging her nipples over my chest...

"You make me so wet," she confessed into my mouth. "I n-n-need you, Mikey. So badly. I feel ready to explode."

She hadn't been a talker the last time we were together but damn...

Her words...

Was Molly a dirty talker?

It turned me the fuck on.

Dirty, kinky sex wasn't part of my past. Could it be part of my future?

Whatever it was, I was never readier to sink into a woman's body than I was right then.

Never had a moment been as all-consuming as this one right here.

I pulled away from her mouth, dropping my mouth to her neck. "Tell me more, Moll." When I bit gently, her body did that same full-bodied shiver she did earlier in the night, and her nipples tightened more against my chest. I could now feel how wet she was against my slacks; the moist heat against my hard cock an aphrodisiac.

She'd been turned on at the Gala.

That was what those little shivers of hers were.

"I want to ride you. Right here. Like this," she confessed, dropping her head to the side to allow me more access. I licked up the column of her neck until I could take her earlobe into my mouth, biting gently. "This...this all-consuming need..." She said the same words I'd been thinking. "Just like this."

CHAPTER FOURTEEN

MOLLY

This was not me.

I wasn't a flower petals and champagne girl either, but I'd never experienced this powerful need.

The moment the words echoed in my mind, I knew it was true.

All-consuming.

Frantically, I brought my hands to the fly of Mikey's slacks and he was kissing my neck again—my neck, my shoulder, my collar bone—until finally I had his pants undone and open. He didn't stop as I reached inside his briefs, my hand coming into contact with his hard, steely length.

I lifted up on my knees then, as I pulled his hard cock away from his body. Mikey slid his hands closer to my core and that small movement had another rush of need pooling between my thighs.

When the fingers of his hand slipped into my folds, my thighs clenched hard. The tip of his finger came into contact with my thong, but the smooth material didn't stop him. He swirled his finger around my opening before moving my thong aside.

I tipped my hips, brushing the head of his cock through my wetness before bringing the bulbous tip back. When I slowly sank down over him, our answering groans were in unison.

My head dropped back as I fully sat on his lap, taking a moment to adjust to the thick fullness of him. Mikey kissed the center of my neck, then dragged his teeth to the side, leaving another kiss there. His hands tightened on my ass and I began to roll my hips over him, the hard ridges of his cock brushing against my softest walls in the most intimate way possible.

I'd taken him bare.

He was in me without any protection.

I gasped and stopped. "You're not—"

"I'll pull out," he told my neck. I didn't understand how we'd had the same thought at the same moment but...

"Move, Moll," he demanded, his hands pushing at me until I did just that. "You feel so good. Too good. Shit, Molly. I've got you. I'll protect you. You're fine. Just move."

I kissed him again; my hands were on his face and his were on my ass, and I rode him like I needed to. Fast. Hard.

Mikey's mouth muted my moans, and soon, just by the fullness of Mikey's cock inside me, I was close to coming.

"More, Mikey," I demanded, my rolls and lifts from him in small, short motions.

I felt more than saw Mikey slouch back, allowing a different angle. Now, every time I rolled over him, my clit made a glorious rubbing contact with the short, manly curls he had over his pubic bone.

"Oh, God," I murmured, but the heightening of sensations only had me moving faster, more frantic to get to the edge.

"Yeah, Molly. Show me. Take pleasure from my cock. You're so fucking beautiful." His words were low, the tone one I'd not heard before, thick in his desire.

Then, after pulling me forward to rest on his chest, he brought his mouth back to my ear, the soft feel of his breath sending shivers through me. "I love you, Molly."

And I was thrown over the edge.

I squeezed my arms around his neck as my body convulsed in my orgasm, my thighs quivering and my hips jerking as, just when I thought I was over the best of it, his cock twitched and sent me over again.

Then he was standing and carrying me, his full, pulsing cock still between my thighs. With each step he took toward his room, his fullness brushed in all the right places. I moaned into his neck, squeezing my eyes shut. Something about your eyes being closed, heightened all the feelings.

In his dark room, he lowered us to the bed, his body not leaving mine. He was kissing me again, this time slower. I hooked my feet at his back, enjoying every moment.

Soon though, he pushed away. For one quick moment, I was afraid he'd changed his mind.

That he got me off and was done.

But when I looked down the bed to where he stood, I saw him simply removing the rest of his clothes. And the look in his eyes…

Maybe it was the dim lighting from the living room, barely filtering into his bedroom, but the look in his eyes…

God, Mikey looked like he wanted to devour me.

There was a gentle nudge in my head, one telling me to get up and follow suit, so I did. I pulled myself off the bed and, because my dress was already undone, the material simply fell from my body.

I hooked my thumbs into my thong, but Mikey shook his head. "Lay down."

I lifted my brows, but he only mirrored my expression, a look of amusement managing to break through the raw desire in his eyes.

I sat at the edge of his mattress, keeping my eyes locked on his, before moving so I was near the head of his bed, not a trace of awkwardness in me.

This is right.
Right.
Right.
Right.

With a devilish look in his eye, Mikey followed me, his body a hard masterpiece as he crawled up the end of the bed. I wantonly spread my thighs but, before he could move directly over me, he knelt between my legs. He brushed his hands slowly over my thighs, rubbing his thumbs over the move sensitive insides.

His hands…

The man's hands were magic on my muscles. I was equal parts relaxed as he worked my muscles and turned on as he drew his hands closer to my pussy.

"I can't wait to taste this," he mumbled, his eyes surprisingly still on mine. I would have expected him to be looking down at me, figuring out his next course of action, but no.

He was looking right at me.

"Taste your desire against my tongue. Feel your thighs tighten against my head. You okay with that, Moll?"

I was so okay with that, I was salivating for it. I simply nodded though.

Mikey lifted my legs until my feet rested on his chest. I curled my toes and when he began to tug on the light-spandex of my no-show thong, I used his chest as leverage as I lifted my hips.

He brought the material to my knees, then leaned back so he could pull them fully off. Mikey kept a hand on my right ankle though, keeping one leg in the air as I dropped the other to the bed. Then, he turned his face in a began a trail of kisses from my ankle, to my knee, gently lowering my leg to the bed as he moved to lay between my open legs.

I reached for another pillow and put it behind me, wanting to watch as much as I could.

I wasn't a stranger to the whole 'going down' thing, but I could say that it wasn't a particularly mind-blowing experience. It felt good, sure, but I preferred to watch my lover take satisfaction from my core—that was the part that made it better for me.

Don't count him out, my thoughts laughed.

If anyone would make it worthwhile, I had a feeling it was Mikey.

He kissed my inner thigh and slowly, as if he were savoring every moment, parted my lips before dragging his tongue up from my center to my clit, where he swirled his tongue right around the bud.

Oh.

My eyes closed, squeezed tightly, and my body arched from the bed.

Yes, oh.

I forced my eyes open again and caught him watching me. I couldn't see his mouth, but his eyes were clearly smiling. Then he did it again, and I stretched my legs out long, but that caused my pelvis to tip down.

No good.

I brought a knee up and Mikey continued his licks and sucks, his tongue swirling around my pussy in a zig zap pattern here, a circle there...his tongue dipping inside me and moving quickly. He kissed, he sucked, he swirled.

And soon I was on the edge again.

So much for this not ever being a particularly mind-blowing event.

Mikey knew what the hell he was doing.

"Mikey..." I whispered, closing my eyes again, giving in to the sensations. I didn't need to see him to reach my peak.

Just feeling him...

Feeling his lips and tongue and teeth...

And then they were gone.

Just...gone.

My eyes snapped open and I groaned my disappointment.

I watched as he leaned his strong, muscular body away from me and toward his nightstand, where he pushed aside both pairs and single socks. A bundled pair even fell out of the drawer as he frantically pushed around.

"Shit, c'mon," he mumbled, and I had to smile.

Then, because he left me on an edge, I tried to give him a taste of his own medicine and reached for his straining cock. His abs clenched when my hand squeezed him, and he growled when I brought my thumb to the crown, coming into contact with the wetness that seeped there.

"Molly," he warned, as I swirled the drop of precum around

the head. "Thank fuck," he said a quick second later, pulling out a square foil packet.

I let go of him so he could roll the condom in place. I wanted to feel him lose control in my body. I couldn't *wait* to feel it. And that was the only reason why I let him go so easily.

Condom in place, he moved from his knees between my legs, to beside my legs. I frowned but then he tapped my hip.

"Roll over."

I lifted my brows.

"Please."

"I don't—" I started but quickly stopped myself. I didn't exactly enjoy being gone down on pre-Mikey, but he made it so worthwhile. He would probably make doggy style more exciting that I had experience with too. That thought in my mind, I rolled away from him, exposing my backside to him.

I got up on all fours as he helped move my legs apart, settling between them again. His hand rubbed appreciatively over my right ass cheek. Dropping to my forearms, I looked over my shoulder at him.

I looked like a fucking dog in heat—my ass up in the air. But I quickly put the thoughts to bed, because Mikey?

Mikey looked like he enjoyed the view.

"Beautiful," he murmured, as he kneaded my ass. I couldn't help but wiggle a little; I needed to feel him inside me again.

He chuckled. "Impatient," he said softly and then, oh my God, he slapped my ass.

My mouth dropped open and he just grinned over and down my back at me, his hand rubbing away the sting.

"You slapped me!" My voice was incredulous; I'd never had dirty, kinky sex before. I'd never thought spanking could be a turn on but...

"Spanked. For being sassy. You're so fucking sassy, Moll." Before I could offer a retort, his hands were splitting my ass cheeks and then he was pushing into me from behind. I dropped my head, my temple to my forearm, and pushed my hips back into him. "And stubborn. So fucking stubborn."

I opened my eye but kept my head down, as I glared back at him. "Not stubborn."

He was smiling—it was wide, amused, and a touch cocky. "Stubborn. And you passed it on to my kid. I see you in him every damn day." He began to thrust his hips and I moaned.

"Let's please not talk about Anderson right now," I managed, my eyes closing again.

"I'm just sayin'," he said, pausing after pushing in all the way. "You belong here, Moll. Right here. In our lives. Don't go."

I wiggled my hips, needing him to move. He was big and wide inside me, stretching me, and I needed more. And he wasn't giving it to me.

"Not going anywhere, Mike," I finally growled after he refused to move.

Mikey laughed, "There she is." And then he spanked my other ass cheek.

This time, it wasn't shock that coursed through me but more need. My pussy squeezed around him in response, surprising me.

"Ah, you like that, do you?"

I braced myself for him to do it again, but he didn't. He smoothed his hand over the spot then grabbed my hips, beginning a quick but even thrusting.

It felt so good.

So, so good.

I pushed up on my hands and arched my back when he grabbed my hair, pulling gently. He pulled a little more until I rose up on my knees, kneeling in front of him with my body arched, his hips relentless as he continued to drive his cock into me.

He wrapped his arm around my middle, holding my there for a moment while I moaned with each push of his cock, each lick of his tongue over my shoulder. He kissed and licked and moved, and soon, dropped his hand from my stomach until his fingers were brushing over my clit.

The second they did, a shiver ran through my body and I moaned loudly. He began rubbing my clit in circles and I needed something to hold on to. Reaching up and behind me, I held onto the back of his head.

He rubbed, and circled, and flicked...

"Oh my God," I moaned, trying to tip my hips back more. I was already arched to my max.

But I needed more.

So, I told him that.

Soon, we were laying down, me still to my stomach and him over my back. His fingers never left my clit but his other hand dragged down my arm until he locked his fingers over mine, clutching them tight as I tried to keep purchase with the sheets under me.

Even with his hand trapped between my body and the bed, he didn't let up on my tight bundle of nerves. Instead of circling though, he moved his fingers over, back and forth, until trapping my clit between two fingers.

And then he squeezed.

"Mikey!"

My body convulsed under him, my fingers tightening against his as I squeezed my eyes shut. He didn't let up on the pressure around my clit until my body began to calm down.

And then he was pulling his still hard, still pulsing with need, cock from my body, and I groaned.

He rolled me over and I eyed his covered cock, obviously in need of release. Why hadn't he come yet? Why could I get him almost there, but not *fully* there?

I brought my eyes up to his and could feel the frown on my face. I didn't want the answer but... Still, I had to ask, "Do I not do it for you?"

CHAPTER FIFTEEN

MIKEY

Molly's body reacted so strongly to mine.

The fact I now got her off twice—and hell, could have been three times had I let her come against my mouth—made my chest puff out in pride.

That feeling quickly deflated at her question though.

"What?" I asked, moving to lay down beside her. I needed contact and, for the time being, resorted to keeping my hand on her stomach.

"I mean, you…" She didn't touch, but instead pointed to my aching cock. "You haven't…"

"You think I can't come to *you*, is that what you think?" I pieced together.

"Well, yeah. I mean, it was one thing to hold back in the living room but here?" Her temper was starting to flare from being unsure. "I mean, what's holding you back? Me?"

After all these years knowing her, in one single night I was pulling out the many intricate pieces of Molly Attwood and learning who she was, completely, in and out.

I knew she called me Mike when irritated.

And I knew she had a sarcastic, stubborn side.

But now I was seeing how closely these things paired with

her being unsure.

I'd set out to give her as much pleasure as I possibly could. I wanted her to see how good this side of life could be. I wanted her to crave me as much as I craved her.

I didn't intend to make her question my desire for her.

"No, Moll," I answered, conscious to not smile at her. If she saw I was laughing at her, I knew her enough to know she'd only get more irritated and fuck, but I wasn't knocking one off in the shower to my hand.

Not when the very reason I was hard—and had been hard—was right here in my bed.

She opened her mouth, but I moved in to kiss her hard. She mumbled against my lips but after I moved my hand up her stomach and cupped her breast. After I kneaded it lightly and tweaked her nipple, her mouth softened.

Only then did I pull back away.

"No," I said again. "Trust me, baby, I can get off to you just fine. Have been for years," I admitted simply to see the shock on her face. *Yeah, Molly, are you catching on?* "I wanted you to feel how good it could be between us. This is you and me. All of this. You bring out these desires in me." I continued to mindlessly work her nipple, rolling it slowly between my finger and thumb. She shifted slight, just enough to show she was turned on again. Still. "You have a dirty mouth—"

"Never before you," she managed around a moan and I realized I was squeezing too tightly. Didn't need her too close to the edge again. I loosened my fingers, keeping them light as they brushed and rubbed her sensitive peak.

"Yeah, can't say I've spanked someone before. You brought that out. Not gonna lie, I liked your response," I chuckled, still watching her.

Her eyes were darkened by the dilation of her pupils and damn me, I wished I'd had the foresight to turn on the lights when we walked into the room. The dimmed lights of the living room weren't enough.

But I also wasn't leaving this bed.

"Don't do it every time," she answered, her eyes closing again as her body slightly arched.

We were going to do this again.

This wasn't a one-night deal.

This was going to be different than the last time.

I didn't think it was possible, but my cock hardened even more. So much for my grand plan of keeping her over aroused. I wasn't going to last this time.

"We good?" I asked, squeezing her nipple this time on purpose as I dropped my mouth to kiss beside her lips.

"Yeah. We good," she repeated, and I smiled at the improper phrase coming from her lips.

"Good." I kissed her again and this time, moved over her. She wrapped her legs around my hips and I wasted no time pushing inside her. This time though, unlike the living room and when I took her from behind, I pushed my hips into her slowly, pushing her into the bed, hard, when our pelvises met, flesh to flesh.

This time was slow, and sexy, and sensual.

Her hands ran slowly up and down my back, my sides.

My hands…one was in her hair, cradling the back of her head against the pillow as the other ran up and down her thigh.

This time was perfect, and I knew—as deeply as I knew my place in life, my place in the Perri's and Gagnon's lives, and my place as Anderson's father—this was where I was supposed to be.

Where we were supposed to be.

I chose Molly.

And shit, she chose me.

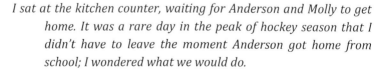

I sat at the kitchen counter, waiting for Anderson and Molly to get home. It was a rare day in the peak of hockey season that I didn't have to leave the moment Anderson got home from school; I wondered what we would do.

We could go somewhere.

"This is a very nice place." The slight French accent had me

turning in my stool. In the middle of the living room, her fingers turning ornaments on the tree, was Trina. "You did well." She smiled over her shoulder at me, her blonde hair even more gold in the sparkle of white Christmas lights.

"You don't think it's too much?" I asked her. "It's nothing like our first place."

She shook her head, looking back to an ornament with Anderson's second grade picture on it. I knew that one well. Anderson was missing one of his top teeth, and both front teeth on the bottom. His hair was also a crazy mess because of a scheduling conflict with the second-grade class and the school photographer.

"Well, you're a different hockey player than you were then. That, and this place is still modest, Mikey," she laughed, reaching for a different ornament. That one, a ceramic pair of skates that Molly hard written on the bottom, "First year playing! 2011"

Trina looked at me again, her eyes dancing. "Why am I not surprised?"

"He's good."

"Of course, he is. You're his father." She looked back at the tree again, taking it in, before moving toward me. "You have no pictures in this house, Mikey."

"Sure, I do. There are some of Anderson in the hall."

"Why not pictures of you with him? Molly with him?"

I looked past her, into the hall that lead to his and Molly's rooms. The hall that pictures of Anderson decorated the walls. "I don't know. He has a picture of the three of us—you, me, and him—in his room."

"Molly has pictures of her and him on her phone. You should tell her to print them. Then put them in the house."

"Molly—"

"She belongs here, don't you think?" Trina asked, moving to sit in the stool beside mine.

I nodded. "I do. She belongs here..." My voice softened to a whisper.

"Then show her that!" Trina laughed, pushing at my shoulder. "I mean, I feel her here. She has a very special energy, my friend. But I was expecting to see her in these walls. Why haven't you put her here?"

"It hasn't been easy, Trina. There were some bad days, and then there was a boyfriend, and..."

"And she always came back when I pushed her," Trina said, matter-of-factly. "She's not very great with subtle hints, though. Molly is very literal and very honest. The few times I've visited with her, she insists we talk about the past but you, Mikey, you let me talk about the future."

I laughed lightly at that, looking away from Trina and to the counter as I nodded. "I always listened to you."

"Why don't you listen to her?"

When I looked at Trina, her head was tipped to the side as she studied me. "I listen to her."

"Yes. Now. But you didn't always. She'd been telling you for years that she loved you—" My mouth opened to cut in, but Trina continued, "and that she needs to be here, but you never saw it."

"She never said it."

"Sure she has. Maybe not in words, but she's shown you."

I hadn't seen it. She'd also never said it. "I don't know that Molly loves me. Not yet."

Trina just nodded her disagreement. "She does. She's afraid

though."

"She shouldn't be. I don't plan on going anywhere."

"You're her family now, Mikey. Molly won't risk that—"

"Trina. I know. She and I have talked."

"Oh. I must have missed that conversation," Trina replied before shrugging. "Can't be everywhere."

"What's kept you here?"

"A soul has to be sure her loved ones are doing okay before leaving them."

"And Anderson and I weren't doing well?"

"Andy is doing fabulously."

"He doesn't like Andy," I interrupted, and she just rolled those blue eyes of hers at me.

Funny, I couldn't remember her being an eye roller, but Molly...Molly rolled her eyes all the time. For a moment, I wondered if that had been Trina. The thought was crazy.

Then again, I was talking to my wife.

"Like I said, Andy is doing fine. He's loved and he knows it. He wants you and Molly together, did you know that?" Of course, Trina didn't let me answer that. "So if any of your hang-ups are on him, don't worry about our boy. But you and Molly... I just want to see you two happy. Ten years is a long time, Mikey." Trina's voice turned to a sad tone. "A really long time. You have so much to offer someone and Molly is so good for you. Why do you think I chose her?"

"You chose her?" I asked, confused. That sounded eerie, like Trina always knew she was going to die.

Trina shook her head, smiling again. "No, I didn't know I was going to get into the accident, silly. People don't know those things. But I always knew Molly was special. I love her and wanted you to love her too. There's no one better for you than Molly. She's better for you than I ever was."

"Trina..."

She nodded. "She is. She'll keep you on your toes. You need that, Mikey."

I couldn't help but nod too, because Trina was right. Molly was good for me.

"The last time we talked, you forgot our conversation," Trina said then, her voice firm. "You need to remember our conversation."

"We've talked?"

"Yes, a couple years ago, love. It takes too much for me to visit you, so I generally just try to whisper to you, but I'm tired, Mikey. Please remember this conversation. Please be happy. She's going to wake up soon, so please remember." Then, she reached for my face, her hand light to my cheek even though the action oddly felt like a kiss to my side. "I love you, Mikey."

With the feeling that this was the last time I'd say the words to her, I smiled. "I love you, too, Trina."

CHAPTER SIXTEEN

MOLLY

I woke up slowly.

The room was dark—at some point after I fell asleep, Mikey must have gone into the living room to turn off the lights. I lifted myself up to look over his sleeping body to see the time.

Only four.

With a sleepy sigh, I lowered myself back to the bed, cuddling into Mikey's side.

Last night had been…

Incredible.

That was one word for it.

Hooking my leg around his, I slowly dragged my foot up and down the inside of his calf. I didn't want to wake him, so when he sighed heavily in his sleep, I stopped moving my foot and instead, curled my arm over his flat stomach. He slept on his back but had an arm under my neck; I could imagine him holding me close before he'd fallen asleep and relaxation took his arm from around me.

I moved my hand to the left side of his chest, searching the strong beat of his heart. It was slow and steady as he slept. I kept my hand there for a while, counting the beats until my eyes grew heavy again.

I remembered his words from the night.

All of them.

The dirty ones.

The sweet ones.

And the three words that when strung together…

Just thinking of them had my heart swelling and stuttering again.

Mikey loved me.

And it wasn't just words. It was evident in the way he took care of my body all night long.

Tell him, that little voice in my head urged.

Well, if anything, telling him now would be easiest, wouldn't it? When he was asleep?

It would be like practice.

I rubbed my hand softly over his pec, then side, still feeling his heart against my palm. I thought the words.

I love you, Mikey.

Mikey, I love you.

I love you, Mikey Leeds.

The words terrified me.

Saying them made them real.

Saying them meant that if he ever decided he didn't feel the same way, I was going to be alone.

Life is about experiences, Doll.

I frowned at the words in my head but understood their intent.

Life wasn't meant to just exist.

It was meant to be experienced.

You had to do the scary things in order to appreciate the beauty.

So, after swallowing back my fears, I pressed a kiss to Mikey's side before whispering in to the dark, "I love you, Mikey."

But it was his sleepy answer that had me knowing, once and for all, no matter how he denied it…

I would never be enough.

CHAPTER SEVENTEEN

MIKEY

Molly was gone, and I couldn't get ahold of her.

Eight days.

Eight fucking days, and *nothing*.

No call. No email. No fucking text.

Just *vanished*.

She didn't even answer Anderson's questioning text, which really pissed me off.

The longer she was gone, the more my anger grew.

No, not anger.

It was disappointment that I felt.

What happened?

I replayed that night no less than one-hundred times in my head, and I couldn't figure it out. Everything about that night was great.

Everything.

Until I woke up in the morning to another fucking disappearing act.

As badly as I wanted to dwell on it, I couldn't afford to be upset at the world.

I committed to playing tomorrow.

I *had* to play on the anniversary of Trina's death.

When assistant coach Deacon "Draz" Drazenovic came to practice yesterday, announcing that Ryleigh Prescott had passed away the night before—thankfully, shortly after the boys got to her—I stepped up to the plate. Without the Prescotts, and with Winski out, the team needed me.

It wasn't likely that any of the Prescotts would be in San Diego for the game, and I couldn't very well fail my team because of a superstitious hang-up.

But I was having a hard time keeping my disappointment in Molly from taking over every other thought in my head. She occupied my thoughts during the day, and my dreams at night.

How could she...?

Why?

Just, *why*?

I pulled my phone from the pocket of my jeans, pulling up her contact card and hitting the 'text' button.

Not for the first time this week, I shot off a message. *Talk to me.*

A few of the messages, I'd started out angry and it came across in my words. I knew my anger wouldn't do anything but push her stubborn...*ass*...further away. So, I made my words nicer.

I added 'please' a couple of times even.

But still, nothing.

Sighing, I flipped my phone over. It wasn't like she was going to answer me, at the rate the week had gone.

I heard Anderson come in through the garage—he'd asked to ride the bus this week—and I turned on my stool, momentarily hit with this sense of sitting here once before, turning to face the tree...

I shook the feeling off and waited for my son to come through. When he did, he threw his backpack to the couch, not saying anything even though he looked at me.

"How was your day?"

Anderson grunted a non-reply as he walked toward me and straight into the pantry.

I could learn to be okay with Molly leaving me, but I was having a hard time wrapping my head around the fact she willingly left Anderson too.

After all her talk about not wanting to leave him...

Shit. I knew it wasn't talk when she said it, which made her silence all the more confusing.

What.

Happened?

Anderson came out of the pantry with a granola bar and pack of fruit snacks, avoiding my eyes. I let him, watching as my son moved around the kitchen.

Molly's voice echoed in my head as I watched him. *"Don't you wonder what he would be like if he knew her? What of hers he'd have picked up on?"*

Anderson was a result of his environment and while he looked like me, with his mom's blonde hair, Anderson had so much of Molly in him. If Trina hadn't died, how long would we have kept Molly around? Would we have had more kids? Would Molly have married Curtis, leaving us, because Anderson had Trina?

If Trina hadn't died, the question wasn't so much *what of hers would he have picked up on*, but more, *who would he be without Molly*?

If she was gone for good...

Shit.

If she was gone for good, I'd still *see* her every damn day in my kid.

"Have you talked to her?" Anderson asked softly, his back to me as he reached for a water glass.

"No, bud."

He turned around quickly, worry sketched on his face. "This isn't like her! She's never not talked to me. *Never*, dad! What if she got in an accident? Like mom? What if...?" My boy didn't finish his thoughts before his face crumbled. He killed me.

I was out of my stool and to him as quickly as I could, holding my ten-year-old close as he cried into my chest.

"I know, Anderson," I murmured softly, my hand in his hair. "I'm trying to fix it, bud. I'm trying. I just don't know where she is."

He sniffed hard and pushed back, looking up at me with

glassy eyes. "Did you go to her apartment? You didn't, did you?"

What little faith my boy had in me.

"I did, Andy."

Twice a day; on my way to the arena, and on the way home. She wasn't there.

I didn't know where she was.

Didn't know why she couldn't at least answer Anderson.

The thought of her being in an accident had crossed my mind a time or two, as well. Who would know? If she did get hurt, who would authorities let know? Anyone? Or could she be in a hospital somewhere, alone?

I didn't like those thoughts.

I pushed those thoughts aside.

"Maybe Asher knows where she is!" Anderson's face cleared. "Molly would have told her. She has to know. Did you ask her?"

"I..."

No. I didn't think to talk to Asher.

Which was stupid of me. Of course, she would have talked to Asher.

They were friends; probably the only true friend Molly had. *Like Molly had been for Trina.*

The thought of Trina had my mind fighting to remember something, but again, I shut it down. I had to figure out where Molly was.

At least to be sure she was okay.

I would never forgive myself if...

Hell, she just had to be okay.

The previous twenty-eight hours had been hell.

Asher finally responded to my text nearly six hours after I sent it—Yes, she knew where Molly was, but she didn't want to be found. Yes, Molly was "okay"—and she used quotes, so I knew Molly really wasn't okay. But I didn't know how to fix it.

How did you fix something when you didn't know what was wrong?

I hated trying to get information out of Asher, especially knowing all of the Prescotts were still out in Wisconsin. So, after I dropped Anderson off at Winski's for him to hang out with him and Callie, I shot another text to Molly, even though I knew it would go unanswered.

Hell, at this point, maybe even unseen. *I miss you. I'm sorry, Molly. Please just talk to me.*

And then I put my phone away for the night, forcing myself to focus on the game.

I hit the bikes, trying like hell to pay attention to the televisions.

I hit the shower, going over plays in my head.

I threw on my gear and tapped my pads, thinking mindless bullshit: *over my head, strap, strap; up the shin, strap, strap. Peel tap, attach behind leg, around, around, around, around, tear. Lower shin, around, around, around, tear.*

Forcing myself to think about steps to do something, at least kept my mind off—

No. Not thinking about her.

Then, just like every year before, I stepped out onto the ice during warm-ups okay. The trick would be walking to the locker room before the game began. It was always then that the nausea set in.

I skated around the zone, taking in the crowd before lining up for our first warm-up drill. Rocking back and forth on my skates, I waited my turn, all while the guys around me talked.

The veterans of the team knew to leave me be.

The rookies must have been told to do the same.

When drills were through, after we did one last group one to get the puck past Kirby McDuffy in the net, I took myself off the ice. There were still three minutes left, but I needed time to decompress.

Draz, going over notes on his clipboard, glanced up at me as I walked into the room. "You good?"

I swallowed past the need to throw up and nodded. "I've got it." I would push through this stupid hang-up.

The worst thing that had ever happened to me on this day was Trina's accident.

And that was nine years ago, today.

Nothing bad would happen.

Nothing bad will *happen.*

I am going to be fine.

"The boys look up to you, Mikey. You're doing a good thing tonight."

"As long as I don't croak on the ice," I mumbled to myself, walking to my stall and sitting back, closing my eyes and focusing on my breathing.

It wasn't long before the rest of the guys piled into the room too, and Draz started going over plays and our major line changes. I listened, even though I was bent over with my hands over my face, fingers pressing into my eyes and needing to remind myself to breathe.

"Alright, let's go play hockey," Draz announced and, one last deep breath, I put my fears to rest.

It was just another day.

Another day to play hockey.

My first face-off was rough, but I quickly got into my groove by the middle of the first period. By the end, I found myself with an assist—Fitz made the goal—and I was mostly relaxed.

As relaxed as a guy could be while playing hockey at the minutes I put in.

The night was going fine.

I lost the urge to puke, and I was playing almost normally.

I was afraid to think it but maybe I'd finally managed to put my fears to rest.

It was my seventh shift of the night—the period was almost over and I was ready to have put a third of the game behind me.

"Leeds!"

I looked around the ice for our open man, the puck in front of me. I was aware of Vegas' guy coming at me from my left, and the guy trying to get around Travers to my right. I was looking for the one who called my name.

"Leeds!" Nash's voice pulled through the sounds of skates on ice, and the crowd chanting and cheering. Moments before I was plowed into, I released the puck in Nash's direction. I got an elbow to the neck, the jab feeling like someone was choking me, but fuck if that shit was caught and called.

Damn blind linesmen.

Nash passed off the puck to Little D'Amaco who slapped it toward goal the moment it was in sight. His angle was off slightly, but Nash pushed around the Vegas defender who was on his ass, and—beautifully—sent the puck home.

Just as the period buzzer rang.

"Yeah!" Nash yelled, his arms in the air. Me and the other on-shift skaters rushed him, hugging and slapping his back and helmet, before we made our way back to the bench, Duffy not that far behind us.

The atmosphere in the locker room was up, but Draz ran a different ship than Caleb, and talked business the moment we were all seated in our stalls.

"Good first period, boys. We had a few weak spots though..." I listened to him with half an ear, throwing back a fruity protein shake. "One down, two to go. Keep up the energy," Draz finished, just as Mulligan and our equipment manager, Jeff Troy, walked in. Troy immediately went to grab skates that needed sharpening and Mulligan went to Draz. I turned toward Big D'Amaco beside me.

"You hear from Porter?"

Nico nodded. "Yeah. On accident. The babies Facetimed me." He chuckled. "Porter was forced to talk to me when he realized it. He said it's fucking cold and the wind was making his eyes water. Except he was inside when we were talking."

I couldn't help but grin, even though I knew the heartbreak those boys were going through. Mom or wife, the hurt was real. "The wind, was it?"

"Yeah. He 'fessed up to it a few minutes later though. Asher had a really close relationship with his mom, so I honestly think

Ports is trying to be strong for her."

"You think—" I started, but Draz called my name. "What's up?"

He waved me over and I frowned at Nico before standing, making my way to where he and Mulligan stood. The medical trainer's eyes shifted, and a terrible feeling washed over me.

Molly.

Anderson.

"What's wrong?" I managed to say without my voice breaking.

Draz, his face tight in a frown, sighed heavily. "Anderson's in the hospital."

CHAPTER EIGHTEEN

MOLLY

"Are you home yet?" Callie asked, the moment I answered my phone. There were only a handful of people I was answering too, and while I wasn't incredibly close to Callie, I still liked her enough to answer her phone call.

"I've always been home?" I was confused. I hadn't gone anywhere.

Well, I'd been staying at Asher's while they went out of town. Watched after their giant dog, Caine, for their family so they didn't have to board him.

"Oh. No one knew where you were. At least, Mikey didn't know where you were."

Yeah.

He didn't.

I didn't want him to.

Not yet.

Not while I was still trying to get over the last tear to my heart.

And it killed me to not talk to Anderson, but I really just needed a little bit of space before I figured out how I was going to move on.

Again.

I couldn't believe he'd called out her name...again...

Just like every other time this week, the thought of those last moments brought tears to my eyes. Like I told him, he could never love me like he loved Trina, and whatever love he thought he had for me?

It wasn't enough.

"How's Trevor doing?" I asked, forcing my mind away from Mikey.

"He's okay. He's learning to deal with the fact he's not going to play anymore. We talked about getting an emotional support dog for him. Okay, well, I talked to him about it. He's not completely sold on it, thinks it's hocus pocus, even though I've told him I've seen these dogs work magic but anyway, I had a reason for my call." Her voice was starting to sound rushed, and it concerned me.

"Is everything okay?"

"Mostly. Um. So, we have Anderson tonight while Mikey's playing. And he had a bit of a freak accident." My heart stopped in my chest, but Callie continued talking. "Do you maybe have guardianship or has Mikey given you caretaker rights? I've got him here at the hospital, and he's in the back being X-rayed, but I think he'd do better with someone with him. I mean, he's doing fine! He's in good spirits, but I really hate that he's back there alone."

"Oh my gosh," I finally said, moving to stand from the couch. Caine lifted his heavy lion-like head from his place on a giant dog-pillow, tracking my movements with curiosity. "Yes. I can be there. I'm at the Prescotts' house. Porter and Asher's. I can be there in, I don't know, fifteen minutes? Twenty?"

"Okay. Good." Callie sounded relieved. The woman had been a pediatric nurse! Her tone worried me.

"Is it bad?" I asked, slipping on old-school sweater clogs.

"Oh my goodness, I've probably worried you. I'm sorry. It's just a bad break. I mean, there's no 'just' to a broken bone but—"

Relief rushed through me, but I still rushed out of the house, alarming and locking it, and got into my car. "Okay. Good. I'll be there."

"Molly!"

Anderson's face lit up when I walked into the room. I slid the glass door back to the position it had been in before opening it and walked over to him.

As soon as I got to the pediatric Emergency Room, I talked to Callie and sent her home, before being directed to Anderson's room. The doctor would be in shortly.

"Are you okay, bud?" I asked. When I reached him, I automatically ran my hand through his hair, my eyes falling to his splinted arm. "What happened?"

He sighed, rolling his eyes. "It's so stupid. I was chasing Dylan and Colt, then tripped on a toy." He tried lifting his arm and winced.

"No, don't move it."

"Anyway. I caught myself funny and *snap*! Just like that. Snapped in half."

He sounded proud, while me? The thought of my bone just "snapping" in half sent my stomach rolling.

"Then we got here, and they gave me some medicine, and I feel fine."

I couldn't help but smile at him. "They gave you the good stuff, did they?"

"What's the 'good stuff'?"

I laughed lightly. "Not the Motrin I give you for your headaches and molars."

"Oh. Yeah. Real good stuff." He nodded a few times, then settled back into his pillows. "Callie called the team. Dad's going to blow."

Shit.

It was the twenty-third of December.

The day didn't even register in my race to get here but...

"He'll be fine," I tried reassuring Anderson, but he shook his head.

Anderson's mood changed from upbeat to melancholy like the flip of a switch. "No. He had to play tonight. Because of me, my dad is never going to play again."

My stomach was rolling now for different reasons.

Mikey played tonight?

He got on the ice, and played tonight?

Everyone knew that Mikey's one superstition, was he couldn't play on this day…and he did, and look what happened?

"He'll be fine," I said again, even though I feared he wouldn't be.

The door slid open and I turned my attention to the person walking in, wearing Marvel scrubs. I looked for her badge, then saw the RN tag sticking out from behind her identification card.

"Hey. I'm Steph. I'm Anderson's nurse."

Anderson nudged me. "She likes Thor. I told her that Iron Man was the best."

I smiled down at him. "I think Thor's pretty awesome too." I brought my attention back up to the nurse. "Hi, I'm Molly. Anderson's nanny. I'm in his chart."

Steph nodded. "Yes, I did see that. We'll be setting his arm shortly, but do you think Anderson's father will get here soon?"

I looked at the clock. Without knowing when Mikey was called, and where he was in the game… "I don't, I'm sorry. I do know he was contacted."

"Okay," Steph said with a smile. "Well, Anderson, how are you doing? Need more ice chips?"

Anderson shook his head. "No, thank you. I'm okay right now."

"Alright. Then, I'll be back in a little while." She quickly jotted something down on a piece of paper she pulled from her pocket then left after another quick smile to Anderson.

"Ice chips? That's fancy," I joked to Anderson before pulling a chair to his bed.

"I can't eat anything right now," Anderson pouted. "Callie was going to make giant ice cream sundaes for me and her, after the boys went to bed. I purposely didn't eat a lot of dinner, so I'd eat the whole thing."

I laughed, shaking my head. "Only you, kid. Only you…"

We settled in then, turning on the wall-mounted television and finally agreeing on the Disney channel. Anderson stayed quiet during the show, but the moment the commercials came on, he looked over at me.

Gone was his happy expression.

"Why haven't you been home?"

With a sigh and a tight partial smile, I reached over the bed and grabbed his good hand. "I'm sorry, bud. I needed time to think. Just grown up stuff." It had been cowardly of me; I knew it when I quietly left the Leeds house, but hearing Anderson's sad tone just drove that thought home.

Cowardly.

Selfish.

"We missed you."

Part of me wanted to fight that comment—*Anderson* missed me maybe, but Mikey? He missed the idea of me. Of having someone there.

Not me.

But another part of me...

He misses you too, Doll. So much.

That odd feeling washed over me, much like at the gala when I heard the small giggle. And Doll...

Only one person in my life ever called me Doll.

Moll-Doll.

Molly-Doll.

And that was Trina.

Thinking of Trina...

My eyes began to water at my betrayal.

At my thoughts last week that I could be happy with what had been hers.

He loves you.

I shook my head and swallowed hard, my eyes focusing on Anderson again. "I missed you too, Anderson." I reached over with my other hand to ruffle his hair, and registered his eyes widening before I heard the door slide open again.

"Anderson." Mikey's voice was breathless, and maybe a little bit wild.

I removed my hands from his son, and stood, ready to face Mikey. I braced myself for the onslaught of hate, but I should have known better.

Mikey stood there, taking in his son in a hospital bed, as I took *him* in.

He looked worse now than he did nine years ago, coming out of the airport—as if this day, this last hour, had aged him.

He hadn't even bothered with his dress shirt.

Mikey looked like he tore out of the locker room in a rush. His slacks were on without a belt. One of his dress shoes was untied. And his undershirt tee wasn't tucked in.

"Just broken, dad. I'm sorry," Anderson's voice came from behind me. "It'll be okay. The nurse was here, and she was cool with Molly but wanted to talk to you before doing anything major with my arm. You think I can get a green cast?" Anderson took the role of adult, and gave Mikey the major rundown, while all I could do was just stare at his father.

Mikey's eyes shifted then, landing on me.

I was expecting his face to close off.

For him to immediately turn his eyes away and ignore me.

Hell, for him to *dismiss* me.

I was not expecting the man's face to fall; his eyes watered, and his jaw slackened, as if seeing me gave him permission to break.

My heart tripped in my chest; I didn't know what to do. I was frozen in my spot.

Thankfully, I didn't have to do anything at the moment, as the doctor came through the door right after Mikey.

"Mr. Leeds. I wasn't sure you'd be able to make it so quickly. I'm Dr. Schwimmer. I'm with Orthopedics."

Mikey tore his gaze from me, cleared his throat, and turned to the doctor. As badly as I wanted to watch Mikey and hear what the doctor had to say about the plan, I gave Anderson company.

"Green, yeah?" I asked him.

"It's the best color," was his answer. "Bright green. Neon

green."

"That's pretty bright."

Anderson gasped. "Do you think they have *glow-in-the-dark* green?!"

"If not, I'm sure we can make it happen with paint or something."

"That means you're gonna come back to the house, right? Will you come to Christmas with us? Dad's no fun on the plane. He just wants to sleep, and sometimes the plane doesn't have the best movies. I think you should come," Anderson went on, his rambling no match for me. I wouldn't be able to cut in if I tried. When he was on a roll, he was unstoppable. I let him talk, listening to him and enjoying his words.

I'd missed him.

I'd missed his father.

"Alright, Anderson," Dr. Schwimmer announced, which finally had Anderson quieting. "You ready to do this thing?"

Anderson's face finally fell completely, and he resembled a scared ten-year-old, rather than the happy, chatty one he normally was. "Is it gonna hurt?"

Mikey walked over, taking a spot on the other side of the bed. "You've got this, bud." He leaned down to press a kiss to Anderson's forehead, and I made myself turn away from the show of emotion.

Mikey still looked like he was ready to break into a million little pieces, but he managed to hold himself together, ever the strong one.

"There's a waiting room outside of Ortho that you guys can stay in, or you can hang out in here," Dr. Schwimmer said, hitting a button on the wall. Only a few seconds later, and two new nurses came into the room, followed by Steph with a big blue chart.

I looked to Mikey; Anderson was his son. Whatever he wanted to do...

"We'll come with."

We.

I swallowed hard and forced myself to meet his eyes. He held them—*one Mississippi, two Mississippi, three Mississippi*—then forced a smile at Anderson. "Let's do this."

CHAPTER NINETEEN

MIKEY

Draz had offered to get someone to give me a ride, but I told him I was fine.

I nearly had a nervous breakdown in the cinderblock hallway though, making my way to the car. It was there that I turned on my phone—something that was far harder to do than someone would think.

Trevor and Callie left messages.

The first, a voicemail saying Anderson had fallen and caught himself funny, breaking his arm—to which Trevor said it was clearly a clean break.

Then, text messages with updates from Callie.

Including one that said she got ahold of Molly.

It was that one that allowed my heart to slow down from its race; allowed me to calm down enough to get to the hospital without adding reckless driving to my list of accomplishments.

Seeing her in the room with my boy...

Shit, it was the rock that crumbled the dam, and if it weren't for the doctor, I probably would have made an emotional embarrassment of myself.

She was okay.

She was here.

She was okay.

I didn't care about anything else. Didn't care that she'd left. That she'd been a ghost.

She was here now, and that was all that mattered.

We followed behind the medical team as they rolled Anderson in a wheelchair out of the ER and toward ortho. One of the nursing staff showed Molly and me to the waiting room. Unfortunately, nearly every seat was taken, but for a single one near the corner.

"You can sit," I told Molly. There were a couple doubletakes as we moved to the back of the room, but none of the parents or kids said anything. It made little difference to me if someone in this room leaked that I was at the Children's Hospital; the team would have to release a statement anyway, with my leaving in the middle of a game.

She shook her head. "You probably need to sit more than I do." Her voice…

Once again, the emotions in my body began to build. The day, the notification, the call, the texts…

I collapsed down into the chair and didn't think twice about reaching for Molly's middle, pulling her close, and pushing my face into her stomach. I didn't cry tears so much as silently sob, my shoulders shaking, as I held her.

When her hands threaded into my hair, I squeezed my arms around her tighter.

She held me, as I held her, her fingers moving through my hair in gentle, soothing motions as my body shook with the pent-up emotion of the night.

After another moment to calm myself—and with the lingering thought that these people probably thought my kid was dying, with the show I was putting on—I pulled my head away from Molly's stomach. Her hands still in my hair, she stared down at me, her face stoic, but her eyes…her feelings were evident in her eyes.

Without a word, I moved my hands to her hips and pulled gently; she let go of me and willing allowed me to guide her to my lap, where I just wrapped my arms around her again, pressing my face to her shoulder.

We sat there in silence, but the moment didn't call for words.

Her being her was enough.

...But would she stay?

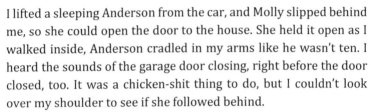

I lifted a sleeping Anderson from the car, and Molly slipped behind me, so she could open the door to the house. She held it open as I walked inside, Anderson cradled in my arms like he wasn't ten. I heard the sounds of the garage door closing, right before the door closed, too. It was a chicken-shit thing to do, but I couldn't look over my shoulder to see if she followed behind.

In theory, she'd have to—the mechanical door sounded before the regular door—but part of me was afraid she was going to leave again.

It was that part that had me carrying Anderson to his room and avoiding the fact that Molly may be gone again.

I tucked my son into bed after removing his shoes. He'd be fine in his clothes.

Clothing was going to be the least of his worries when he woke in the morning, his arm in pain. The doctor said his meds wouldn't likely wear off until around five, and even though he gave us a stronger narcotic for the first few days, I wanted to try regular, over-the-counter pain relievers before breaking out the hard stuff.

He was probably going to be more upset about the fact I cancelled our flight to Quebec, than about his deep green cast and the pain that lived behind it, anyway.

Leaving his door open a crack, I headed back toward the middle of the house, where the lighting in the kitchen was dimmed. I could hear Molly rummaging around in the cupboards and when I cleared the hall, saw her standing on tip toes in front of the cabinet that housed meds and prescriptions. We kept things placed on the second shelf when Anderson was younger, so he wouldn't reach them.

Funny, Molly could hardly reach them herself.

How had I never noticed that?

I took a moment to watch her, and after she pushed aside a box of band-aids and an orange prescription bottle, I went over to help.

"What are you looking for?" I asked, standing directly behind her.

If anything, she went up on her tip toes further. "There's a grape liquid Tylenol up there somewhere."

I reached over her, moving another bottle. She dropped down to the flats of her feet, and I found the bottle she was looking for, adding it to the small pile she assembled.

The liquid Tylenol, as well as two different flavors of chewable Motrin.

Molly turned then and, avoiding my eyes and instead focusing on my shirt, she said, "He usually responds to Motrin better, but he's never had something of this magnitude. You may have to alternate them, to keep on top of his pain. Like the doctor suggested. He likes the chewable Motrin; don't bother finding the chewable Tylenol. He doesn't care for it."

I stared at the top of her head, as she told me how to care for my boy.

Where would we be without Molly?

Dammit, why didn't she see that she *belonged* here?

I feel her, but I don't see her.

I frowned at the memory—or whatever it was—but it was true.

I felt Molly in this house.

But she didn't exist. Not on the walls. Not for the world to see.

"Molly."

She stopped talking but didn't look up. She did, however, take a breath that had her shoulders slumping forward.

Tired of being a coward, and aching to feel her skin again, I cupped my hands on either side of her face and tipped it up, forcing her to look at me. Her lips tightened, and it was only a matter of seconds before her eyes took on a glassy sheen.

"Talk to me," I whispered. "Please."

She shook her head in my hands.

"I don't know what I did, baby, and it kills me to know that something spooked you. Why? What happened, Moll?"

She tried to cast her eyes downward, and knowing I wasn't going to get anywhere—yet—I changed tactics. "Thank you for being there tonight."

"Of course, I was," she barely managed to whisper. I dropped my hands from her face, gently kneading her shoulders, my thumbs brushing circles under her collar bone.

Behind me, on the kitchen island, a phone buzzed. I was going to ignore it, but it buzzed again.

With my hands still on Molly's shoulders, I looked over my shoulder, spotting her phone. The screen was lit up, and her screensaver was a picture of her with Anderson.

Molly has pictures of her and him on her phone. You should tell her to print them. Then put them in the house.

Trina's voice was clear as day in my head.

Confused, I looked back to Molly, who was also looking toward her phone, but the expression on her face was tired.

"It's been acting up," she mumbled, shrugging from my hold. "Goes off for no reason. Must be time for a new one."

Still confused, feeling the frown on my face, I reached for Molly's hand. "Molly? Why did you leave?" I felt the nudge to ask, as if her answer was more important than I realized.

"Mikey…" she said, obviously tired.

"Why did you leave?" I pushed again.

With an exaggerated look to the ceiling, she sighed heavily before shaking her head, "Because I told you I loved you and, in your sleep, you told Trina you loved her. Like last time. You won't ever love me, not at the same capacity you loved her. And I don't have it in me to compete with that."

In a rush, my dream of Trina came back to me.

As well as her sweet, sure words: *There's no one better for you than Molly.*

"That's…" I shook my head, trying to clear it but trying to find a way to tell Molly what I thought had happened. "Moll, it's crazy, but I had a dream about Trina that night."

Molly stepped away, picking up her phone and turning off the screen, blacking out the image of her and Anderson. "I'm going to head home," she answered, and I could hear how upset she was.

I needed to make her understand.

"Not like a dream, but like she was talking to me. She talked to me, Molly. Said she talks to you too."

Molly offered me a sad, almost pathetic smile, and shook her head. "Okay, Mikey."

"No. Listen, Moll. Please. Just listen."

"You can't love me like you loved her!" Molly finally broke. "Not how I love you," she added her body finally shaking as she gave in to what she clearly thought was a breaking heart.

That wasn't how I wanted to hear her tell me she loved me.

And I'd be damned if that was the only time I heard it.

I pulled her close to me again, and she didn't push back.

She also didn't wrap her arms around me, keeping them to her sides.

That was okay. I'd hold her enough for both of us.

I held her tightly to me as I bent my head, talking low in her ear. "I love you, Molly. So damn much. And I know without a doubt in my soul that Trina would approve of us. I *promise* you. I'd told Trina I loved her in my dream, and it felt like it was the last time. I swear, Moll, if I ever do it in my sleep again, you have permission to wake me up and slap me, but fuck, I don't want you to doubt what I feel for you.

"I love you so much. This week has been hell, with not knowing where you were, and you not talking to even Anderson. Hell. Please hear me."

We stood there in silence.

The longer she said something, the bigger my fears grew.

She couldn't trust what I'd said.

She would still leave.

And then she confirmed that thought.

"I have to go."

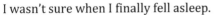

I wasn't sure when I finally fell asleep.

Whenever it was, I knew I'd only have a couple of hours before pain would likely wake Anderson up, so trying to sleep was important.

And when I did wake?

I had a dog at the end of my bed that didn't belong to me.

And my girl wrapped in my arms.

CHAPTER TWENTY

MOLLY

I drove to Asher's, completely drained.

Driving in the dark, exhausted from the day and emotions, likely wasn't my best idea, but I couldn't remember the last time I'd let Caine out.

Mikey's words echoed in my head.

I wanted to believe them.

So badly.

Doll, you believe them. Trust yourself, love.

That voice in my head…

I shook it off.

However, it was still bothering me as I stood on the back porch, waiting for Caine to finish his business in the yard.

I thought back through the years.

Every time I returned to Mikey and Anderson, it was more than Anderson's text.

It was this overbearing—hell, *irrational*—feeling that I *had* to be there.

The times I put it off, those times I managed to stay away for longer than a week, my anxiety attacks were almost debilitating. Life would finally calm down when I gave in to the push.

Other than the push…

Her laugh, at the gala.

When Mikey told me he loved me.

That was Trina's laugh.

The words in my head, my thoughts calling me *Doll.*

Was that Trina?

It was crazy, but I allowed myself a moment to think about it. Was Trina pushing Mikey and me together? Curious, I pulled out my phone and, thankful internet searches weren't monitored— allegedly—I typed in *visits from the deceased.*

The first result had my eyes tearing up as I read through it.

Maybe it really was Trina all along.

Go back. They need you sweetheart.

I looked up from my phone, my eyes wet with tears, as I nodded into the late-night sky. "Okay."

A sense of calm washed over me, right after one last French-tilted laugh.

With a tightness in my throat, I tried to work back the tears and sting in my nose. "Okay, Trina."

"Shh," I whispered as Caine bounded into the house. The once tired, oversized dog was nowhere to be found, and in his place was a one-hundred-and-fifty-pound ball of energy. Apparently, Caine enjoyed car rides. "It's bedtime."

Caine stopped in the middle of the unknown living room, looking around.

For his equally oversized pillow, I was sure.

"Come here," I whispered and, after slipping out of my clogs, walked quietly through the quiet ranch house, toward Mikey's room.

Soft snores came from within, and I hoped we wouldn't wake him.

He needed the sleep, and I wouldn't bet money on Anderson sleeping past five-thirty.

"Quietly," I whispered as we neared the end of the bed. I tapped gently and, surprisingly, the dog climbed up with grace, laying down without much movement to the bed. I slipped out of my leggings and, in just my tee from the day, climbed in beside Mikey.

I curled into his side, staring at his profile in the dark. He stopped snoring, taking a deeper breath. A new wave of his sleep cycle.

With my hand over his chest and over his heart, I tried again—not that I was going to wake him up and hit him.

I'd save that response for the morning.

"I love you, Mikey," I whispered.

He shifted in his sleep, sliding his arm under my neck and pulling me close. His voice heavy with sleep—and with another rumble of snores shortly after—he whispered roughly, "Love you, Moll."

EPILOGUE

DECEMBER 23RD

MOLLY

"He's going to kill me." I fidgeted nervously in the cinder-block hall, looking around at the ones who were here for support. For me, or for Mikey, I wasn't so sure anymore.

The brown, Kraft paper bag in my hand was going to lose its handles, if I kept playing with them, my nerves fried. I refrained from putting the bag on the floor though. I needed something in my hands.

"He'll be fine," Sam answered, wrapping an arm around my shoulders and pulling me to his side. We all wore 'Leeds' jerseys, every single one of us: Luc, Marie, and Sam Gagnon all in the deep forest green jerseys the men wore here at home usually as well as Trina's mom and dad—the true emotional sucker punch, and I wasn't going to blame hormones on that one—who wore auctioned jerseys from various events through the years.

I was starting to feel faint, but Sam shook my shoulders in his hug. "Calm down, Moll. It will be good."

Anderson, who stood with the Perris—drowning in Mikey's auctioned holiday jersey from last year—smiled over at me, his eleven-year-old face filled with mischief and still a hint of that young awe.

"Yeah, mom. He'll be ecstatic." Then, he looked over his shoulder to his Mamie. "I had to write a story for English class, and the emotion I drew from the hat was ecstatic. It means really excited."

Marie smiled and bent down to kiss her grandson on the forehead.

I watched the exchange with a lump in my throat.

These emotions, man…

Mikey and I married in late summer, and while we *invited* the Perris—they were family, after all—I hadn't actually *expected* them to come.

I was taking what had been their daughter's.

I was taking their daughter's place.

…All thoughts that were quickly put to rest when Adele pulled me aside before the small outdoor wedding. *"She wouldn't have wanted a different outcome for her boys."*

Between her words, and the memories of what I chalked up to Trina talking to me, I felt okay.

Better than okay.

"Who told me this was a good idea?" I murmured, getting nervous again. The last thing, the *very* last thing, Mikey needed after this game was an urgent text message. "This was such a bad idea. So bad."

"Too late to fix now, sis," Sam quirked, the smirk on his face only adding to the fact he found this whole thing funny as hell. He sobered quickly though, squeezing my shoulders to him once more. "He needs more positive on this day."

And that right there, was why I foolishly concocted this plan.

Last year, the first year he managed to get on the ice for the team's last game before Christmas break, and it had been tainted by Anderson being in the emergency room. At the beginning of this season, Mikey swore he'd be able to play tonight's game, but the closer we got to December, then to Christmas, the more I could see my husband battling with it.

I needed him to see the day in a different light.

So, I told everyone in this hall my plan, and they all thought it was brilliant.

That's what Sam said, anyway.

The sound of steps echoed through the halls, a heavy-footed person rushing through on his way to the garage; my breath caught as my heart began to pound.

It had to be Mikey.

It was going to be Mikey.

"You've got this," Sam whispered in my ear before releasing me, stepping back to join the parents. Now, Anderson stepped up, standing beside me.

He, too, was fidgeting with his fingers.

"We got this," I whispered low, moving my hand from the roped handles to the top of the bag, no doubt crumbling it with my nervous grip.

"We got it," my adopted son's voice was just as low as mine, but sure in tone. If there was only one person who was completely behind this reveal, it would have been Anderson.

The footsteps neared and soon...

I took a deep breath as Mikey rounded the corner, frantic worry over his face. His eyes were wild, his hair a mess, as if he half-assed his shower and threw on his clothes after the game. His tie was around his neck but not knotted.

He looked like a man in a hurry.

When he focused his gaze on what was in front of him, his steps faltered, his face morphing into confusion.

"What...?" He stopped, but only for a moment. Soon, he was walking slowly toward Anderson and me, his face...

"I thought...?"

He stopped directly in front of Anderson and me, his hand automatically going to brush against my hip, then sliding more, to rest on the small of my back. Even through the thickness of material of my own replica jersey, I could feel the slight tremble in his hand. "Everything's okay?" The worry and fear in his voice was palpable, and it only added to the nerves wracking through my own body.

"Surprise?" I finally managed to find my voice, even though it cracked. My thoughts and emotions were working overtime.

He looked down at me, to Anderson, then back at our family. "There's..." he swallowed, and I could see as the panic slowly receded from his eyes, "no emergency?"

At the persuasion of Sam, I may have text my husband that he was needed at the car *as soon as possible!!!!!!!* After the game. Which, Sam followed up with his own urgent text message.

"But Coach said..." I felt Mikey's fingers dig in briefly against my back.

I may have also gotten Sydney Prescott in on the plan.

"So, what's..." Again, his voice trailed off, confusion overriding the fear now.

"Tell him!" Anderson nudged my side, and I looked down at the boy I'd known since he was a baby. A boy I had the pleasure to watch grow up, to mother, even though he wasn't mine by blood.

A boy who knew about Trina, loved Trina, but still chose to call me his mom.

"Yeah, Moll, tell him," Sam goaded from behind me.

I threw a playful glare over my shoulder, and in the process, saw our family waiting excitedly.

"Tell me what?"

I looked back and up, to see Mikey staring down at me. His full lips were parted slightly, just enough that I could see the lower edge of his upper teeth.

I took in the rest of his face. His straight nose, his green eyes; the light freckles that his son had in spades.

All qualities I hoped would be passed on.

My lips tightened as I swallowed nervously, and Mikey's eyes dropped to my lips as my tongue darted out to wet them. "Um."

My husband's hand dropped to my ass—covered in buttery soft leggings—and I was pretty sure he was copping a feel before he grabbed hold of the bottom hem of my jersey.

"Moll?" His eyes searched mine, and the confusion was still evident.

The words wouldn't come. I couldn't spit them out.

So, instead, I thrust the now crumbled brown bag at his stomach, making him grunt with the force. His hands left me to grab the bag and, curiosity etching over his features, he separated the top, peering inside.

His green gaze immediately popped up to mine.

Mikey opened his mouth to say something, but Sam beat him to it. "Well, what is it?" he asked, even though he knew damn well...

His mouth worked, words not falling from his lips, and he looked back down, a hand timidly reaching inside to pull out the gift, the bag dropping mindlessly to the ground.

In my husband's hand was the smallest 'Leeds' replica jersey I could find. It had to be custom made, and was sized for a toddler, but it would keep...

His eyes searched mine again. "Are you...?"

I nodded, my eyes filling with tears.

"You're not shitting me?" His voice was filled with wonder, and I shook my head, trying to smile but it only caused tears to spill over on my cheeks. Even through the tears, though, I could make out his blinding smile.

Suddenly, his arms were banded around me, lifting me off the ground. I wrapped my own arms around his neck, burying my head into the crook as he did the same. The wetness of his tears brushed my neck and I could feel his entire body trembling—adrenaline, excitement, and maybe even a little leftover fear.

"Fuck, I love you." His words were muffled by my body, and I squeezed my arms around his neck tighter.

"Congratulations, man," Sam broke in. Even I could feel the strength behind his back pounding.

Reluctantly, Mikey lowered me back to the ground and, jersey still in hand, wiped at his face with the back of his hand. His other not leaving me.

"I hope it's a boy, but I guess a sister would be okay," Anderson piped in, stepping close to our circle. Mikey pulled him to his side, his arm around his son's neck.

"You knew about this?" he asked him with a smile.

Anderson nodded, grinning. "I did. We kept a good secret, didn't we?"

"Yeah, you did." Mikey leaned down—not nearly as far as once upon a time—and pressed a kiss to the top of Anderson's head. The excited seventh-grader's age came out then, as he tried to duck away, but still, with a laugh.

Even though everyone else in this hall had known and congratulated me already, the sentiments and hugs were plenty, for both Mikey and me. When it was Adele's turn to hold Mikey in a close embrace, I overheard her tell him the same thing she told me in the summer—and again, my eyes began to burn.

With a sniff, I stepped away from Mikey and into Luc's arms. There wasn't any room for tears; just smiles and laughter.

It was later, much later, with the Gagnons and Perris settled in at the hotel rooms, and Anderson in his bed, that Mikey pulled me back into his chest. I tipped my head back, the smallest of smiles on my lips, as I looked at our giant Christmas tree—decorated and with presents hiding the skirt, ready for our Christmas Eve celebration the next day.

I'd decorated this very tree more times than I could count. It was one I shopped with Trina for, for Anderson's first Christmas. The branches were starting to look sad, from years of bending and remolding into place. It was probably the last one we'd have with this tree.

For years, I'd hung Anderson's handmade ornaments, and keepsake ornaments that had been gifted to him and Mikey. For years, I'd wrapped the extra strands of white lights, and climbed the ladder far higher than my fear of heights allowed, just to put a star at the top.

For years, I'd done all of that for a pair of boys I loved with all my heart, but never thought could be mine.

And this Christmas...

This Christmas, they were.

And they always would be.

"Thank you," Mikey whispered into my ear, his linked hands resting on my stomach. I cuddled further back into his body, my sweatshirt and his thermal no barrier for the pounding of his heart at my back. "I didn't think it could be possible," he added before pressing a kiss to my temple, "but you made a bad day more than bearable. This was the best Christmas ever."

THREE YEARS LATER

MIKEY

"Anderson!" My wife's whispered yell sifted through my nap-fuddled brain.

"I just wanted to tell dad before I left," our son whispered back.

"If you wake up your sister…"

My grin was slow, and as badly as I wanted to stretch, my hot-box of a daughter was still cuddled to my side. Little Miss Peri Kate was a warm sleeper—something that terrified her mother and I on more than one occasion when she was smaller; fevers in newborns, and all that came with that.

I opened my eyes then glanced toward the bedroom door, taking in my wife and son, before trying to carefully dislodge myself from my octopus of a daughter.

Peri slept one of two ways—completely spread out, taking up the entire bed; or clinging to you like a monkey.

She took up the entire bed when she'd sneak in at night to cuddle, which these days, wasn't too terrible because Molly left plenty of room in the bed, while stuck on her left side—if she even managed to sleep.

Or, during pre-game naps, Peri would cuddle right into my side.

Sure that my daughter was going to keep sleeping, I rolled out of bed and finally stretched, my eyes squinting toward the two in the doorway.

Anderson was getting taller every day; he'd been taller than Molly for nearly three years.

Molly…

Molly looked tired, and ready to pop.

"Sorry," Molly whispered, her eyes moving to land on the bed.

"I was awake," I semi-lied, whispering myself. When

movement sounded behind me, I stopped, frozen, in place.

Everyone stood still.

I was pretty sure everyone held their breath…

And when Peri's little sleep moan sounded, the one that said she was falling further into her dreams, there was a collected, yet silent, sigh.

Our two-year-old still needed two naps a day, but on game days, we pushed her past her morning nap in hopes she'd take a longer afternoon nap. She'd still fall asleep at the game, but she wouldn't be a bear when she was awake.

Before we could step out of the bedroom, I put my hands to both sides of Molly's nine-month belly, leaning in to press the smallest of kisses to her lips. Her sigh was happy but still…tired.

When Peri made her entrance to the world, Molly had been a tired, sleepless zombie for forty-eight hours before her water broke.

It was only a matter of time…

Hell; hours even, maybe.

"You okay?" I asked against her lips, pulling back just slightly to take in her brown eyes.

Molly nodded. "She's comfy." Her hand brushed over mine before rubbing at the top of her swell.

"Could be a boy," I countered. We didn't know what we were having, but there were bets.

Molly was convinced the baby was a girl—her entire pregnancy acted nearly identical to her pregnancy with Peri. Both she and Anderson were betting on pink, and our friends were divided. Peri had her big brother wrapped around her pinkie finger, so how he'd manage another baby sister…

Hell, it was a good thing he had two pinkie fingers.

"Guys. I've got to get ready," Anderson, still whispering, cut in.

With one last check on Peri, we headed out of the bedroom and away from the master wing. This was Molly and my third house—although brief, Molly did live in mine and Trina's condo, before Anderson and I moved into the ranch house. This house…

Well, it was probably bigger than we needed, at six-thousand-plus square feet, but with our Quebec family and hockey family, it was nice having a place that everyone could stay.

All three kids would have their own rooms and bathrooms, and the guest wing—which could be closed off from the rest of the house—had its own kitchenette. Everything still lived on one level; it simply sprawled out and deep, in a giant U-shape.

With my hand linked with Molly's, we walked toward the wide-spread open-concept living area, where, at the custom-built island, I pulled out a stool and helped Molly sit.

"What's the news?" I asked Anderson.

This kid...

Shit, he wasn't a kid any longer. He was fourteen, a freshman in high school, and a first line defenseman on the area U18 travel-competition hockey team, where he played alongside Brandon Prescott.

My kid had more peach-fuzz on his face now than I did at seventeen, and his voice continued to drop.

But when he smiled...

He still looked like my little boy.

"Coach said the scouts at the college showcase liked my playing style!" Anderson's eyes were bright, and his excitement was palpable. "That I could probably play Juniors, or even be drafted right away when I'm eighteen." If there was one thing the kid had dreamed of, it was playing hockey like his old man.

I thought of my own dad, the one I hadn't seen in years. Oh, I'd heard from him, whenever he wanted something, but it was Molly who nipped that one in the bud. Since Molly answered the phone a little over two years ago, he hadn't called back.

She'd been a bit testy at the end of her pregnancy with Peri, I thought with a chuckle.

"Dad!"

"Sorry, Andy. I was thinking." My dad wasn't important, anyway; I had family.

My family was standing in this kitchen—and sleeping in my bed.

My family was scattered around San Diego—players, their families, and even our Quebec family, who were out here for the holiday season. It was Christmas, after all, and while they were told they could stay in the house today, the Gagnons and Perris chose to spend the day out and about.

"That's exciting, right? Can you imagine? Another Leeds on the ice? Shoot, old man, maybe I can play the year you retire. How cool would that be?"

I laughed, shaking my head. "One, you know I'm retiring this year. Two, you're going to college." I moved around the large kitchen island to grab a glass of water.

"But—"

I shook my head, turning off the filter knob and bringing the glass to my mouth, taking a large gulp as I moved back toward Molly. Handing the glass to her so she could finish it, I wiped the back of my other hand over my mouth, shaking my head again. "You're going to college. Too many hockey players get hurt or end their careers, and don't know what the hell to do with their lives. You're going to college."

Anderson's mood deflated a little. "But Dad..."

"Anderson." I raised my brows, my tone no-nonsense. "You're a good player. A great one. That's not going to change because you spend four years playing collegiate hockey. If you do juniors, stay in the states. Play a year. Go to college. Then go pro. You have so many people at your back, you'll play pro." Of that, I had no doubt.

My son grumbled again, and I stepped toward him, pulling him in and pounding on his back as I grinned. "That's really exciting though. Keep playing smart, and you'll be fine."

"I know," he mumbled.

My voice low and for his ears only, I told him words I never heard from my old man. "I'm proud of you." I hit his back two more times before stepping back. "Now, go get ready for your game."

The only bad part to Anderson's U18 schedule was sometimes we played on the same days. Moll and I would pack up Peri, go watch Anderson's first period, then Caleb Prescott and I would head to the arena, our wives and kids heading out after the boys' game.

Anderson grumbled again, but I could see he was fighting a

smile, as he left for his room. Turning back to my wife, I took in her tired expression, one she tried to hide with a smile.

"You going to make it?" I asked, stepping close. Putting my hands on her knees, I pushed them apart gently, so I could stand between them. She shifted in the stool, no doubt her hips giving her issues. She was so fucking uncomfortable.

Which made me feel bad, but also excited.

This baby was coming soon.

"We're good," she answered, a small smile on her face as she tipped her chin up.

I brushed my lips over hers, once, then twice, before grinning. "What do you think? A Christmas baby?"

Molly smiled, but her tone was exasperated. "God, if this baby doesn't come out by the 25th, I'm going to beg for an induction. Heck, a C-section; take this baby out."

Once upon a time, the 23rd of December would come, and I'd be in a fuzz of dread. But once I took in what was always in front of me, once I learned to allow Molly in...

I lived for this day.

Once a day of sadness, it now was a day of excitement.

And today?

Today was the best. The anticipation...

"Are you sure you're good with the games? Maybe you should keep things low-key."

Okay, so I still worried a little on this day, and I probably would only worry more as the afternoon and night deepened.

"We'll be fine. Besides, I'll be with Sydney, Asher, and the kids. We'll be fine," she repeated, no doubt, placating me. Or maybe, she was trying to convince herself. Maybe... "Mike." Molly's voice cut through, and I realized my eyes had unfocused, as my mind began moving at uncertain speeds. "I promise," she said, her hands going to my waist. "We're fine. Now, kiss me before your monster wakes up."

"She has *your* temper. I don't know why you call her my monster," I laughed, as she hooked a foot behind my knee, pulling.

"Kiss me. For real. Or else you'll see that temper."

I didn't need to be told again. Not because I was afraid of her temper; she wasn't that bad. She just stewed quietly, sometimes slamming dishes harder than necessary.

But because I craved her taste.

Her mouth soft against mine.

Her tongue sliding over mine.

Her sighs melting into mine.

With my hands on her face, threading back into her hair, I tipped her face up and gave my wife what she asked for.

I nearly played like shit, constantly looking up to where I knew my family was. Molly made it through Anderson's game—a game they won. And before this game, everyone was down on the Plexiglas during warm-ups, Peri on Anderson's shoulders as she pounded the 'glas above his head, and Molly sitting in a seat.

She looked fine, but I still asked the Prescott wives to keep a close eye on her.

Molly was having this baby tonight; I felt it in my bones. Hell, I was terrified she'd go into labor during the game...not that I told her that. On the way to the IcePlex with Anderson, I'd asked her again if she was doing alright but my wife was convinced the doctors were going to have to cut this baby out of her.

Other than her being tired all the time, and the moments of manic temper, she'd had Braxton Hicks contractions with Peri for an entire week before our daughter decided to grace us with her presence. So, because she hadn't had them yet, she was even more sure she was going to go past her due date with this baby.

I wasn't convinced.

...and because of the ever-slight differences, I was nervous as hell that it would all happen when I was on the ice.

Each rest intermission, I sat bouncing my knee. Nico tried talking to me during the first, but eventually, everyone left me alone. Caleb even assured me, when we walked back to the bench and ice for third period, that if something happened, Sydney would get word to us...

Still didn't help.

Did they not know my stubborn wife?

Hell, she could have been *having* contractions, but because she knew what this day had the ability to do to me, she'd sit there, in fucking pain, holding a baby in.

She'd...

The final buzzer finally sounded, and I stood quickly from the bench, pissed that I managed to make it to the middle and had to wait for twelve of my teammates to make it off. We'd won and were expected on the ice to celebrate and basically wish the fans a Merry Christmas, but I was itching to gather my wife and kids...and be completely sure Molly was still okay.

Hell, I'd welcome being wrong about the baby. Just for today.

As I got to the end of the bench and near the coaching staff, ready to do my duty as an Enforcer and step out on the ice, Caleb caught my eyes and tipped his head toward the tunnel. "Go."

My heart stopped.

"She's fine," he added, chuckling, as I neared. "But I received a message she's uncomfortable."

I stepped to the side to let the other guys through. "Did Moll say it?" If Molly told Sydney she was uncomfortable, that meant this baby was coming now. The stubborn woman wouldn't say something unless—

"No, but Syd says she looks more uncomfortable now, than this afternoon. We're heading home tonight," no doubt meaning Wisconsin, "but call if anything happens."

I nodded, a different set of nerves settling in, and turned away. Caleb backhanded my shoulder before I could step too far away. "Congrats, Leeds."

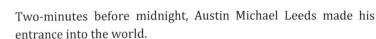

Two-minutes before midnight, Austin Michael Leeds made his entrance into the world.

No cutting required.

Did you enjoy Mikey and Molly's story?
Please consider leaving a review on Amazon!
Also, be sure to check out the Troublemakers: Mignon Mykel's reader group on Facebook!

Continue reading for a look at both
Interference and 32: Refuse to Lose.
The next book to release will be (drum roll....)
Jonny Prescott, with Butterfly Save!

INTERFERENCE

Note: Interference *takes place thirteen years before the beginning of* 25: Angels and Assists.

CALEB

I shouldn't have gone to O'Gallaghers with Jonny last night.

I pulled my pillow from under my head and, face planting into the mattress, pushed the sides as close to my ears as possible. Anything to block out the annoying ring of my cell phone.

Last night, San Diego won. As was tradition, Jon Jon and I went out on the town. Sometimes the other guys on the team would come along but for the most part, it was just me and the kid brother. Back in our peewee hockey days, mom would take us to McDonald's; in college, the one year he and I attended at the same time, we would party in my dorm. Now, we went out, partied long and hard, and of course, shut it down. Most of the bartenders looked the other way with some of the younger athletes in town, and we could always count on Conor O'Gallagher. Rumor had it the O'Gallaghers were a little rough around the edges. Probably why Conor was willing to overlook Jonny not quite being twenty-one yet.

Both Jonny and I had been drafted to the San Diego Enforcers. During my senior year of college, Jonny's freshman year, we both walked into training camp as college kids with great stats, and walked out with spots on the roster. Sure, the Prescott name means something to the organization, but Jonny was a damn good goaltender, and my stats were better than dad's in the respect he didn't touch majors until he was in his mid-twenties, having played in the American league for a few years beforehand.

Last night's win meant the Enforcers were that much closer to Sir Stanley and his Cup. Finals were well within our reach. All we had to do was win Tuesday night's game and we'd make it into the next round. It was a close series, but the odds were in our favor. With Jonny in net, Vegas had to pull all the punches to get the puck past him.

I sighed blissfully when my phone finally stopped ringing, but just as I was about to drop off that sharp edge of sleep, Jonny slammed my bedroom door open. I lifted the pillow enough to look over my shoulder at the intrusion, watching as my boxer-clad brother tossed the cordless house phone onto my bed, bouncing off my hamstring–a little too close for comfort.

"Fucking asshole."

Jonny merely raised a dark blond brow. Oh, the perks of sharing a condo with your younger brother.

I guess it could be worse. My sisters weren't exactly the easiest to live with.

"Next time, wake up and answer your damn phone," Jonny grumbled. "There's a lady on the other end, and I don't think she much appreciated my sarcasm."

I reached back for the phone with one hand as I tossed the pillow aside with the other, before shooting Jonny the bird. As I put the phone to my ear, I watched my twenty-year old brother shuffle back toward his own room. "Caleb," I said on the exhale of a tired sigh.

"Um, hi," came the voice on the other end. Female, like Jonny said. Not high pitched, but not as sexy and throaty as some female voices were. Nervous, maybe. I didn't think I knew her voice, and the landline number was pretty locked down, so she couldn't be some weird stalker chick. I squeezed my eyes shut briefly. Way too much thinking for this hour.

"I'm so sorry that this seems to be an inopportune time. I figured you'd be up and moving, as it's ten." Was it ten already? "I thought that was the time you started practice on game days. I'm on a tight deadline and was really hoping to just leave a message." Ah, she didn't expect to actually talk to me.

"And this is…" I stated, not asked, before yawning.

"I'm sorry," she apologized again. "My name is Sydney Meadows and I'm calling on behalf of Sorenson Media Group. I tried to reach you through your agent, but he directed me straight to you."

I made a mental note to talk to Mark the first chance I got. He really needed to stop directing people to me. Wasn't that his job? To figure out what appearances and gigs were best for his athletes when they weren't doing what they were being paid to do? Fuck, Mark knew I didn't like to sign up for the extra things that came with being a pro-athlete. Events with the team, sure. Gigs at the rink, absolutely. But beyond that, it was a hard no.

"We are putting together a reality television series, and you are one of the names we were interested in having involved with the show," she stated in a rehearsed manner.

I didn't think sleep was going be coming back to me anytime soon, so I rolled over onto my back before throwing my legs over the side of the bed. As I stood, I shook my head. "Yeah, sorry. No reality TV."

"If you'd just let me pitch it to you—"

"That's all you're going to be doing, Miss Meadows. Do you really want to waste your breath? I'm not doing television."

"That's fine," she rushed to say. As she began talking about multiple women and just as many dates, I strode naked to my dresser to pull out a pair of old, worn sweatpants. I pulled them on while listening with one ear. She continued to talk, so I continued to move, walking out of my room and down the hall that was home to both mine and Jonny's rooms, a spare room, and a bathroom, before walking barefooted down the stairs. Whenever she'd pause for an answer, I was sure to give a barely verbal 'mmhm' just so she would continue her rant and be closer to done.

I had sisters. I knew how to work a phone call with the long-winded female species.

"So great," she said finally, with a smile evident in her voice, so unlike the unsure tone at the beginning of our conversation, one-sided as it mostly was. "I will meet you tonight after your game. Thank you so much, Caleb. I promise you, you won't be disappointed."

Standing in front of the fridge now, I frowned when I heard the telltale sign of her ending the call. I pulled the phone from my ear only to stare down at the 'call ended' screen, the frown not going anywhere.

Well shit...

What did I just agree to?

32: REFUSE TO LOSE

TREVOR

"You doing anything Saturday?" my captain and best friend, Caleb, asked as we left hockey practice on a Tuesday afternoon. We'd been playing together for the last nine years and both of us should be nearing the end of our careers…but we were still kickin'.

Kickin' ass and taking names.

We had a game tomorrow night and I was looking forward to having the next twenty hours to myself—the one place where I felt my age showed. All the twenty-year-olds were dying to make an impression, hitting the ice at every moment to prove a point, but me? I'd been with the Enforcers for nine years and just resigned another five-year, multi-million-dollar deal.

I wasn't going anywhere. I had nothing to prove. I'd be skipping the optional morning skate tomorrow, instead keeping the company of a five-year-old girl after school, as her mom put together a custom cookie order as part of her company, *sugar&spice*.

A five-year-old girl and her mom, who just happened to be the daughter and ex-wife of an old teammate.

It hadn't been announced yet, but rumor around the locker room was he was coming back to San Diego. Marlo—my friend and the ex-wife—didn't know yet, as far as I knew. Marlo and Jordan's relationship was rocky, at best, and I was prepared for a full shitstorm to hit when he got into town.

So, I had no problem hanging out with those two tomorrow before my pre-game rituals. As for Saturday, it was one of the rare weekend dates we *didn't* have a game and I was planning on taking advantage of it—especially considering that starting next week, we'd be in a rigorous playoff schedule.

"Relaxing. Kicking my feet up. Pounding back a beer or two or ten."

"Why don't you do it at the house? Most of the family will be in town. Ace graduated."

Ace was Caleb's youngest sister, Avery, and she'd been going to school to be a sport agent. No doubt her brothers—there were three of them total—were excited. "Why's she having the party here?"

"No party. Just hanging out at the house." Then, Caleb slapped the back of his hand at my shoulder. "She's in talks with the club. Wants to oversee a few of the players."

"Yeah. You and Jonny."

"I could talk her into taking you on as a client."

"I like my agent." He always had my best interest at hand. When it came time to renew my contract, I didn't want to fight for millions, but I did want to stay with the Enforcers. San Diego, these men...this was home.

I grew up in a backwoods town in the Upper Peninsula of Michigan and while, yeah, it was nice to go home and be with family...

I liked the West coast.

"Yeah, Cord's a good guy. Not like Mark."

I hated to be the pointer-outer of the obvious but, "If it weren't for his ignoring your media clause, you would not have met your wife."

It wasn't intentional, but Mark knew Caleb wasn't the hockey player who wanted to be the face gracing media. But one day, a little redhead domino named Sydney contacted him about a dating show and rather than dealing with it himself—as an agent ought to do—Mark gave her Caleb's direct number.

They met.

And the rest was history.

There was no one for Caleb after meeting Sydney.

According to Caleb though, the only reason why he didn't drop Mark then was because he knew Avery was going to be a great agent and he wanted to support her.

"Besides," I added, "she'll be too fucking busy with Ports." Porter was Caleb's youngest sibling, the baby of the group—and they were a freaking group, the six of them. Porter, like Caleb and Jonny, played professionally but way out in B.F.N.

Okay, okay, for the Charleston Rockets, out in South Carolina.

Still, though, I'd heard horror stories of that kid and the antics he pulled growing up.

We entered the player's garage and the sound of Caleb's truck roaring to life filled the concrete surroundings.

"Dude, it's not even cold out," I said, in response to his remote start.

"Gotta get her warmed up. Her engine likes it." Caleb winked in my direction and I couldn't help but chuckle, shaking my head.

"Does your wife know you talk like that? That you love your truck more than her?"

"Chief knows she's my number one." Chief was Sydney, not the truck. Not that I would put it past Caleb to name his truck.

"And she knows my mouth and the words that come out of it damn well. Real damn well," he added with a smirk.

"You're a dirty fuck," I chuckled.

Caleb didn't answer, just mmm-ed behind his lips.

Way too much information.

And maybe just enough information that left me envious of the guy. In the nine-plus years I'd known Caleb, he'd been with Sydney for most of them. I teased him once that I had met her first, but he was always quick to come back that if I hadn't flashed her my toothless smile, maybe she would have been interested in me.

Never mind the fact that the only reason why she'd come around was to recruit Caleb for the dating show.

I hadn't stood a chance.

Shit, Caleb really hadn't either, not with how it was supposed to go down, but in the end, it was Sydney he ended up with. She even managed to keep her job as a casting assistant. Now, she was casting all the big shows—and, as much as she grumbled, her best ones were all reality ones.

Hell, I didn't watch much television, let alone reality television, but I made time for the ones my buddy's wife was part of.

In the time I'd known him, Caleb met Sydney, married Sydney, and had her popping out babies left and right. In the beginning, it was funny to watch—Caleb at twenty-five and juggling his first son. Caleb at twenty-seven and his second son.

It was when his daughter was born the following year that the envy started to sink in.

Here I was, in a mix of meaningless relationships—or even relationships that seemed to be going somewhere, only for her to back out—and there he was, having a family and living the life.

"Saturday still stands," Caleb said, breaking away from me as we got to a split in the cars. "See you tomorrow."

By the time Saturday rolled around, I was itching to get out of my place.

We won both our games during the week—further solidifying our seat in the upcoming playoffs—and after a light practice Saturday morning, I ended up caving and telling Caleb I'd be coming over.

It wasn't the first time I'd been to his place when his entire family was over, but the energy never failed to surprise me. Caleb came from a big family so when I looked at his own brood of four kids, it made sense, but being in the house with his siblings and then his own family…it got loud.

In the driveway of Caleb and Sydney's beachy house was a twelve-passenger van.

I literally laughed out loud when I saw the silver monstrosity. Knowing Caleb's family as I did, I wouldn't put it past his dad to have rented it just for the groan factor.

I parked my truck beside the beast and walked into the house through the garage, a bunch of flowers in hand for Avery, and, after walking through their laundry/mud room, entered the open space that made up the living room and kitchen. Throughout the area, were Caleb, Sydney, and their four kids; Caleb's parents,

Ryleigh and Noah, who was essentially the beginning of the Prescott-Enforcers empire; Caleb's oldest sister, Mykaela—who was a hockey legend in her own right, having recently started putting the wheels in motion for a woman's National Hockey Club in the Midwest; Caleb's youngest sister, Avery, the woman of the hour; and Caleb's other sister, McKenna, with her husband and his daughter. Also in attendance, was Caleb's brother, and the Enforcers' goaltender, Jonny, with his wife Jenna, who was talking to some girl I didn't know. I'd been half-expecting to see Porter, too, failing to remember, again, that the kid was old enough to play professionally.

Damn. Knowing Porter was playing pro had a way of making a guy feel old. I met him when he was *thirteen*.

After my small moment of taking everyone in, I walked across the room and handed Avery the bouquet of lilies. "Congrats, kid."

Caleb's baby sister smiled up at me, accepting the flowers. "Thanks, Trev. You know I'm coming after you next, right? My brothers have already agreed to sign once I find a company."

I chuckled at the girl's balls. "And you know I like my agent."

"I'll convince you." Avery nodded, sure of herself—as she should be. She knew the athletic life, the pros and cons of the business, as well as her brothers did. "Give me some time, but I'll convince you."

The thing was—I didn't doubt it.

I looked toward the kitchen to see if Caleb was through with his conversation with Jonny, but it didn't look to be. "Where's your friend?" I asked Avery instead.

"Asher?"

I nodded. I didn't know the logistics of it, but Asher ended up in the Prescott fold at the beginning of the season and what at first seemed to be a few-week thing, turned into something more. The girl had no history, from what Caleb told me, but their mom took her under her wing like a stray kitten.

"In South Carolina."

I lifted my brows, fighting a grin even though part of me was once again kicking myself. "With Porter?" How the hell did the *kid* get a girl, and I was still floundering between relationships?

Avery nodded, smiling. "They're kind of cute."

With that look on her face, I would guess she had a heavy hand in it all. "How much was your doing?"

"This trip, nothing. But maybe a few months ago…" Her voice trailed off as her eyes did the same. Then, she was facing me again, her voice low, to not be overheard. "Jenna brought her sister."

I lowered my voice too, in an exaggerated whisper, as I bent toward her. "I didn't know she had a sister." God, Jenna's parents should have stopped with one kid. Jenna was materialistic. Everything was about show. Money. Whether or not she'd be noticed…

Her parents weren't much different. They weren't exactly the type of people you wanted running the world.

"Caleb wants to set you up."

I frowned, straightening to a stand. "He does not." My voice wasn't lowered this time, and Avery tugged at my arm, bringing me back down.

"Shh! Keep your voice down."

"Ace, Caleb isn't you. Shit, thirty-some-year-old men don't 'set up' their friends at a family get-together."

"Keywords, Trev. Family. Get. To. Gether." She straightened and tilted her blonde head to the side. "Why'd he invite you?"

"Because we're…hockey family." Lame.

"Trust me on this."

I straightened once more and looked back toward the kitchen. Caleb was no longer talking to Jonny and he waved me over, his eyes flashing to his right quickly, where the girl and Jenna were talking.

The girl must be the sister.

She was cute. White-blonde hair pulled into a ponytail. Tiny body. That was the most that I could make out from over here, other than one additional fact. "She's a freaking child," I muttered.

She couldn't be much older than Avery, who just happened to be damn-about ten years younger than me.

Okay, maybe only eight, but fuck.

Jenna's sister was way too young. What the hell was Caleb thinking?

I realized Avery was laughing. "You're really loud."

To prove just that, the girl looked in my direction.

And her cheeks flamed red.

Fuck me.

From across the room, I could see that eyes were a lighter color—I couldn't make out the exact color from here—but I wouldn't be surprised if they were some shade of blue. She looked a lot like Jenna but...

...Sweeter.

If the word could even be applied to a family member of Jenna's.

I turned my back to the girl, trying to get the look of her shock and embarrassment from my mind, and instead face Avery. "I thought we didn't like Jenna," I said, my voice once again low.

It wasn't exactly a secret that Jenna Prescott had very few fans in this room. She was here because she was "family." The Prescotts accepted her well enough, but by her own doing, Jenna distanced herself. The entire time I'd known the Prescotts, Jenna was attached to Jonny, but according to Caleb, Jonny had been a completely different guy before he met, dated, and, eventually, married Jenna.

Avery flattened her hand against my chest, tapping twice with a quick grin. "She's not Jenna."

CALLIE

I don't really know how I got roped into coming to Jenna's in-laws' place.

I knew Jonny's family...*okay*...but I certainly didn't belong at a gathering celebrating the youngest daughter's graduation.

I crossed my arms uncomfortably as I stood in the corner of the kitchen, looking around. Jenna and Jonny—my brother-in-law—just left me standing here. One minute, Jenna was talking to me, and the next, she snapped at Jonny, and they were leaving the room.

I tightened my crossed arms and fought a sigh by puffing out my cheeks. Caleb and Sydney Prescott, the hosts and owners of this very beautiful, yet *modest*—something my sister and brother-in-law didn't know a thing about—home, were pulled apart and talking to different people. I knew Caleb's parents, but they were sitting on the living room floor, playing with their youngest grandkids, Brody—who was one and looked just like his older brothers with dark eyes and bright eyes—and Brielle—who at three, may have been one of the prettiest toddlers I'd ever seen. She had her mom's red hair and a bubbly personality that only little girls managed to encompass.

I turned toward the counter I was leaning on, trying to find something to do.

Shoot, let's be honest, here. Something to *eat*.

I could pass time by eating.

Who the heck knew when Jenna and Jonny would be done doing whatever the heck they were doing, and be willing to take me home. I was supposed to be spending the day with Jenna, planning our parents' thirtieth wedding anniversary. It was the only reason I'd even *gone* to Jenna's.

But my sister literally pushed me back into the elevator of the giant glass building their condo lived in, and said, "We're sending them on a trip to Bora Bora. You owe me five thousand dollars." I'd hardly had the chance to swallow my uprising panic at the dollar signs and she was telling me about going to Jonny's brother's house for something or another.

Essentially, she was holding me hostage.

She knew if I'd been 'set free,' I'd have come up with something else for our parents' anniversary. I knew how Jenna operated. She'd probably just sent off an email to her travel agent when I showed up, and until she knew the plans were in place, she needed me nearby so I couldn't go and derail her plans.

The five-thousand-dollar neon lights flashed in my mind, and I had to fight back the uprising bile.

I didn't even go on vacations for *myself* at that price tag.

Yes, I had a safety net in the bank. But every time it grew over my three-month living budget, I donated it in some fashion—either by direct-check to a charity I believed in, or by finding a mission to fund.

That said, I was currently sitting under my safety net, and

five-thousand for an extravagant trip that my parents would no doubt love…

It was going to send me into a panic attack.

I looked down the counter at the food set out. A Prescott party was so unlike a MacTavish one.

Parties at my parents' had champagne fountains and miles of fondue, with caviar and calamari and lobster topping the menu.

There wasn't bacon-wrapped mini-wienies simmering in barbeque sauce, or homemade Chex mix, or cookies that were most definitely decorated by the ten and under crowd.

I uncrossed an arm to reach for one of said cookies, a circle the looked like it'd had a graduation cap piped onto it, that was filled and decorated in the fashion of a certain Brielle Prescott, if the drawings on the fridge were any indication.

But before I could grab it, it was snatched up quickly from under my nose.

I puffed my breath into my upper lip and changed direction, grabbing a plain, undecorated cookie, before looking up at the stealer of the cookie.

I was expecting Caleb's dad. Or even Caleb himself.

He was neither.

Instead, it was the man who had only an hour ago, called me a child.

I gritted my teeth but refused to appear effected by this…this…monstrosity of a man.

My brother-in-law and the men in his family were all tall, easily over six-foot, but this guy wasn't as tall as them. Maybe only five-eleven.

And he wasn't as lean as the others.

His neck was wide, his shoulders bold.

And his forearms…

I swallowed hard—the guy was serious eye candy in the arm department alone—and brought my eyes up to his.

They were gray. Or maybe just a super light blue.

Then he flashed a crooked smile that showed off perfectly straight, perfectly white teeth. The smile pulled the skin taut on his chin, which brought my attention to a thin, puckered line.

A scar.

"You don't look like you're having fun."

Shoot me now. Even his voice was sexy.

Deep and rumbly, like Sam Worthington when he tried to pull off an American accent.

I forced a smile and waved toward him with my cookie. "Being held hostage. I don't really belong."

He bit down on the cookie I was supposed to be eating, as he nodded. "Yeah." He swallowed what was in his mouth. "At least you're family. In a sense."

I was generally a kind person, but his earlier comment wouldn't stop bouncing around in my head. So, with a frown, I decided to ask, "Why are we doing this? I mean, I *am* just a child." Oh, how quickly I found myself on a roll. I put my cookie back down on the counter, untouched, and held up my finger. "For the record, I'm twenty-two. Legal on all fronts."

His eyes dropped down to my waist and traveled back upward, slowly. When his eyes finally met mine again, he had a smirk on his face and maybe a slight redness to his cheeks. "Still too young."

"For what?" I shook my head. "Never mind." I grabbed my cookie and mumbled to myself, "Shit, where's Jenna? Fuck it, I'll just get an Uber." I didn't belong here. I wasn't a Prescott. And for that matter, the Prescotts didn't much care for my sister, which made my being here even more uncomfortable.

"Waitwaitwait." Then his big paw of a hand was on my forearm and I startled. There was an odd sort of *zing* that went through me and I had to fight from jerking my arm back from him.

Instead, I stared at his large, sun-darkened hand on my lighter skin. When his thumb brushed gently along my arm, I sucked in a breath before looking up at him, tightening my lips.

And swallowing hard.

"I'm Trevor." He paused before adding, "Winski."

I didn't say anything.

"And you are...?"

Still, I remained quiet.

He lifted a brow, which revealed another scar on his forehead, this one in an L shape.

"I'm sorry?" he tried again.

Quiet.

"Caleb's sister told me he was trying to set me up with you. It was a knee-jerk reaction. I'm sorry."

It was hard to stay indifferent at that because that was just ludicrous. "He did not." Caleb hardly knew me and it hadn't exactly been Jonny dragging me along to this house party.

"According to Avery…"

His hand on my skin was making me uncomfortable.

Okay, maybe uncomfortable was the wrong word. That energy was still zipping through me and it was unsettling.

Yes.

Unsettling was a better word.

"I'm being held hostage by Jenna," I finally stated, pulling my arm away. The loss of his hand didn't do much for the energy though. Instead, the large span of skin where his hand had been, tingled. I shook my arm discreetly before crossing my arms over my chest.

Once again, curling in on myself, still uncomfortable with being in this home with people who didn't really know me, yet managed to dislike me because they disliked my sister.

I couldn't blame them. I wasn't the biggest fan of my sister all the time either—our parents' anniversary vacation, a prime example—but she was still family. She was still my sister.

"Did you want to leave?" He almost sounded excited by the prospect.

I couldn't help myself. "Children are taught to not go places with strangers."

"I'm not a stranger. I introduced myself. Something you've still failed to do."

I rolled my eyes as I shook my head. "Fine. Callie."

"Well, Callie. Without sounding too forward and rather as an offer to end your hostage situation, can I take you home?"

FINAL WORDS FROM MIGNON

I can't really tell you when I first thought Mikey was getting a story.

Maybe when he was giving Jordan hell for being a deadbeat dad in 27: Dropping the Gloves. I just knew that I liked the guy, and I wanted to see him move on from Trina.

I *can* tell you the moment I knew he was going to fall for his nanny—

Right away.

Who better for this man, than the very one who stood by his side through the years?

Because this was supposed to be a Christmas offering, that was how Mikey's jersey number came to be, and the whole 'Angels' thing was originally a call out to the holiday.

But one night, while driving home from a night nanny gig (oh yeah, I'm one of those too), listening to Chase Rice's LAMBS & LIONS (Amazon affiliate) on repeat because SAVE ME was Mikey and Molly's song…

Well, my repeat turned into a shuffle, and listening to ON TONIGHT I realized…

THAT was Mikey and Molly's song.

After listening to this song to death, I knew what the ANGEL call-out would be—

Trina.

It then made sense why I was having a hard time writing the

book; I was waiting for my last A-ha moment.

Thank you to my early readers, Jackie and Jennifer. Thank you so much for reading and helping me clear up important points. Your insights were invaluable.

Miss Melissa.

My sound board for this, and pretty much every, story. You listened to me (literally; voice messages on Messenger, all the way) as I tried to figure out how Mikey's story was going to unravel. Thank you for always being in my corner.

To my editor, Jenn. You are a godsend. Honest. You know it, too, and if you don't, let me yell it one more time. I love having you on my team.

To the mignonettes. You ladies rock. Thank you for loving my books enough to want to do your own screaming and promoting, happily reading a book before release and sharing your opinions and thoughts with your reader friends.

Finally, as always, to you, the one reading this.

This month marked my two-year publiversary. I would still be writing if it weren't for you, but it's because of you that I get to call me dreams, reality. THANK YOU!

ABOUT MIGNON MYKEL

Mignon Mykel is the author of the Love In All Places series. When not sitting at Starbucks writing whatever her characters tell her to, you can find her hiking in the mountains of Arizona. Mignon writes in one world, so while every series can be read as a standalone, her stories will be more enjoyable if you read them in publication order.

Also By Mignon Mykel

** The Playmaker Duet (Troublemaker, Breakaway, Altercation, Holding)
can be enjoyed in one easy boxed set.*

Made in the USA
San Bernardino, CA
14 July 2018